THE GLINKOV EXTRACTION

A SCOTT STILETTO THRILLER 3

BRIAN DRAKE

WOLFPACK
PUBLISHING
— EST 2013 —

The Glinkov Extraction

Print Edition
Copyright © 2019 (as revised) Brian Drake

Wolfpack Publishing
6032 Wheat Penny Avenue
Las Vegas, NV 89122

wolfpackpublishing.com

Ebook ISBN: 978-1-64119-635-2
Print ISBN: 978-1-64119-636-9

THE GLINKOV EXTRACTION

CHAPTER 1

Somewhere in New York

IT WAS the kind of murder Siyana Antonova would have done free of charge, except that she never killed anybody without getting paid.

She sat in the living room of a large mansion outside New York City. The property was owned by a rich Russian couple who were hosting a small political fund-raiser. Ravil Zubarev was the guest of honor, a speaker sent from Moscow to bring back whatever donations he could obtain for one of the political parties that opposed Vladimir Putin.

He started his speech with his background and rise in the People's Freedom Party, which often clashed with Vladimir Putin's United Russia Party.

Everybody in the room had once called Russia home, but they'd all left to make their fortunes in America. Siyana felt nothing but disdain for them, bordering on pure hatred. By attending this meeting and giving money, they were conspiring with Zubarev to betray their country and overthrow Putin's administration—not by an election, but by a coup.

Traitors, all of them.

The intended coup had been a recent discovery, and Russian President Vladimir Putin needed to act quickly. The plotters thought they were good at keeping the secret, but Kremlin spies had identified and marked the leaders.

The group couldn't raise money in Russia without risking the whole plan, so they had sent Zubarev, their most vibrant speaker, to visit Russian nationals in the US who were sympathetic to overthrowing Putin.

Zubarev finished his résumé and paused for a moment. Then he said, "I don't like to talk about this next part, because it pains me to see our country having such strife. Kara-Murza and Boris Nemtsov have said that Putin has given us a one-party system, censorship, and a puppet Parliament. And it's true."

The audience grumbled. Several sipped drinks or munched on the snacks provided by uniformed waitstaff. They sipped loudly and chewed loudly. Siyana shook her head. Russians couldn't do anything quietly. They were all dressed well—tuxedos for the men, and various gowns for the women. Siyana didn't have any problem fitting in with her little red dress, which fitted her petite frame very tightly, although she wished the hem was long enough to cover her bony knees. Her elbows were equally bony. To her, they were like balls on sticks, jutting grossly from a mutated freak.

They were the only features of her body that made her self-conscious. Her skin was soft and, now that she had time to regularly visit Coney Island, she was tanned all over. She had thick black hair that fell in a wave down her back, and a bottom some idiot in a bar had once said was as plump as a ripe tomato. The minute he had said it, she'd thought, *Don't look at my knees.*

"If you disagree with Putin," Zubarev said, "you risk prison. Siberia. Exile. Threats to your life and family. If he really hates you, he'll find a way to murder you even if you have left the country. Does this sound like freedom to you?"

The audience responded with a resounding no.

"Is this what we fought for after we kicked out the Communists?"

Siyana folded her arms as Zubarev's voice went up in volume and his gestures became more animated.

The people sitting to her left started whispering, one nodding his head. The others listened with rapt attention.

"We try peaceful protests, and they beat us and arrest us. We try to engage him in the press, and we get shut down, harassed, and vilified. We try to face him in Parliament, but he has people in every corner who are ready to block anything that may loosen his grip.

"There is only one way to defeat this man and give Russia a true shot at freedom, but if we try to raise money in the Motherland, we risk prison. That's why I'm here tonight. We need funds to finance our next candidate's run against the man who is wielding the axe of authoritarianism with an unrestricted hand. We deserve a true chance at democracy, not to have it stolen from us while being told we possess it." He paused, then asked, "Will you give to us tonight?"

Siyana wanted to stand up and say *brekhnya*—bullshit—but she probably wouldn't have been heard over the applause the audience offered, although some were a little slow to contribute. The man was lying because he wasn't sure if he could trust every member of the audience. The doubters. There was still some good sense in the room.

Of course, Siyana knew he wasn't wrong about one thing. Putin *had* ordered his murder.

She raised her head to look at Mrs. Zubarev over the shoulders in front of her. The speaker's wife rose from her chair holding a metal box. What was this, an American church? They were going to pass a collection plate? But that was apparently okay with the audience since the room filled with more talking, drinks and snacks forgotten as the sounds of pens scratching on checks and the counting of cash took over.

Mrs. Zubarev went through the rows, smiling and saying thank you for each contribution. Siyana hated to do it, but she dropped a few bills into the pot as well. To refuse would draw unwanted attention, and she didn't need that. The *shlyukha*—whore—smiled at her and continued down the line. Siyana tried not to visibly seethe. Valeriya Zubarev wasn't wearing a gown but a blouse/skirt/heels combo that made her look like a poor secretary forced to buy work clothes at a thrift shop. Her hair was tied back, she didn't wear much make-up, but the freckles on the bridge of her nose complimented her green eyes.

Her husband was also dressed for business, with a crew cut and a nose that seemed slightly larger than the rest of his head. They were both young, mid-30s, but soon they'd both be dead, and it wouldn't matter anymore. Siyana was the tip of the spear. Once the Zubarevs were dead, the machine in Moscow would spring into action and round up the rest of the traitors in one swift stroke.

ZUBAREV TWISTED off the cap of a bottle of Stoli and poured a splash into the bathroom glass.

"At least take off your coat first," Valeriya chided.

Zubarev exited the bathroom and placed the glass on the dresser. The hotel room was smaller than he would have liked, but at least it was comfortable. He removed his sports coat and hung it in the closet, loosened his tie, and picked up his glass again, then leaned against the dresser.

Val pulled her blouse out of the waistband of her skirt, sat on the edge of the bed, and took off her heels.

"Why are you so tense?" she asked.

"It wasn't enough."

"The money?"

"Of course, the money." He took a long drink and topped off the glass, the bottle going *glug-glug* as the liquor left the spout.

"It will take time. This is only our first stop."

They were working their way up the East Coast. The Midwest was next, followed by a tour through California, then north to Seattle.

Val peeled off her stockings, revealing pale white legs, narrow at the ankles but thicker at the thighs. He found himself staring.

"Litvinenko thought he had time. He's part of the reason we have to act, and soon. We can't waste time. They'll crush us if we take too long."

Zubarev downed the drink and reached for the bottle.

"No more," she said, rising from the bed. Taking the glass, she set it on the dresser. She put her hands on his chest, her long fingernails a shiny pink. She had to look up to meet his eyes, and he felt the heat of her body. He let out a breath.

She was the calming force in his life. They had only been married for two years, having met at a rally where he had been on the sidelines while the party boss gave a speech. She had been in the audience, and they had caught each other's eyes. When she'd smiled at him, a switch had flipped inside him, and he knew he had to meet her. He believed deep down that she was the woman he'd spend his life with. After dating for three years, he had proposed, she had said yes, and now they were working together to restore Russia to her proper glory. He wanted to raise their children in a free Russia, not a Russia controlled by a maniac.

"You need to relax. We have a long flight tomorrow."

"I can't relax."

"What do I need to do to calm you down?"

"Promise the coup will be a success. That Russia will be free."

"You're still giving a speech," she said. "Undress me, and we'll go to bed."

Siyana removed the stethoscope from the wall.

The couple hadn't talked much after their return, but apparently, the night's work had been successful enough that they were extra horny. Pathetic, and a disgrace to Russia all around. The last thing she'd heard after a lot of muffled words and short grunts was Zubarev on the phone, asking for a seven a.m. wakeup call.

Siyana picked up the phone and asked for a six a.m. wakeup call. She occupied the neighboring hotel room. The little red dress had been draped over a chair, and she was wearing a white bathrobe. The room had been arranged via a connection on the staff who was the nephew of one of her boss's captains.

Siyana had been one of the top killers for the Bratva crime family in Moscow, until a run-in with Bulgarian gangsters ended with a price on her head. Siyana's boss had sent her to connections in New York City under the control of Shishkin Pavlovitch, and she'd quickly cemented her reputation in the new land while waiting for the chronically lazy Bulgarian thugs to forget about her. Sometimes she found her gunsights on targets like Zubarev—not criminals or rivals, but enemies of the Motherland. Pavlovitch had a close relationship with Vladimir Putin, and sometimes when Putin needed wet work done, he reached out around the world to Pavlovitch and people like him. Putin couldn't very well send official agents on such matters because he had a reputation as a statesman to maintain. Most of the world bought it, especially a large portion of the American population, who thought him an example of masculine leadership.

The fools.

She put the stethoscope away in a tote bag and decided to hit the sack. She slept with one light on.

Siyana rinsed her mouth with water, stowed her toothbrush in the tote bag, and hopped in the shower. She left the room around a quarter after six dressed in jeans, a t-shirt, a jacket, and running shoes.

The lobby was quiet, only staff members working and getting ready for the morning. The lobby restaurant had recently opened as well. The smell of fresh coffee wafted through the room and she was tempted to get a cup to go, but the job came first. If the Zubarevs woke up early and made it downstairs while she was pouring the milk, the whole operation would be in jeopardy.

Siyana stepped out into the crisp morning air. Clouds hung in the sky. On the opposite side of the wide parking lot full of cars was the freeway. There wasn't much traffic at this hour, but the rumble of cars drowned out any other noise. She couldn't even hear any birds chirping.

She crossed the parking lot, ignoring her car, and climbed into the passenger seat of a white panel van scrubbed of identifying labels. She tossed her tote bag in the back of the van.

A hulk of a man sat behind the wheel. He handed her a Starbucks from the console cup holder.

"You're a lifesaver, Boris."

The big man grunted and took a drink from his own cup.

Siyana sipped her coffee and placed it back in the holder. She enjoyed the warming sensation in her belly after the coffee went down her throat. Under the seat, she found an Uzi submachine gun with the stock folded, and she bent over to keep the weapon out of sight and checked the load. Full mag, chamber empty. She placed the weapon on the floor, rested her right foot atop it, and went back to her coffee. Boris kept his eyes on the front of the hotel. She watched too, glancing at the Zubarevs' nearby rental from time to time.

The rental was a new Chevy Impala, but the souped-up van could more than keep up, despite its extra weight. The suspension had been tuned, and the engine's power boosted as well. Boris, an expert driver, could whip the van around like a six-figure sports car.

Siyana's coffee was half-gone when Zubarev and his wife crossed the lot to the Impala. Zubarev carried their suitcases and loaded them into the trunk. He held the passenger door for his wife and climbed behind the wheel. Such a gentleman. Such a waste of good Russian stock. Siyana wished the man was on the right side of Motherland politics. He was smart and articulate, but for reasons she could not understand, he had chosen to become an enemy.

He started the Impala and drove out of the parking lot.

Boris fired up the van and followed.

"We'll hit them on the freeway," Siyana said.

They followed a two-lane frontage road parallel to the freeway, made a right at a light, and increased speed on the on-ramp. Zubarev stayed in the slow lane despite the light traffic.

Boris merged behind a semi, the van's engine purring. Siyana placed the Uzi on her lap and locked back the bolt. It was two miles to an interchange that would take them east toward the airport. When the semi took the next exit, leaving a gap between the van and the Impala, Siyana told Boris to speed up and change lanes. She powered down her window, and cold air rushed into the van. The hairs on her neck stood up at the sudden chill.

The chill was soon replaced by butterflies in her belly. Her breathing slowed, her chest rising and falling as she breathed deeply through her mouth. Her lips were wet with excitement.

When a sign for the upcoming interchange flashed by, Boris gave the van a splash of power and came up on the Impala's rear quarter on the driver's side.

"Hurry," he said.

But Siyana didn't hear him. She was in her zone, focused on the target. She didn't even unbuckle her belt as she stretched the Uzi through the window, aimed downward, and squeezed the trigger.

Flames flashed from the muzzle, the buzz-saw sound of the fully automatic submachine gun echoing through the van. The rear glass of the Impala shattered, the roof shredded as the hot 9mm slugs ripped through it, and a shift in Siyana's aim brought the final fusillade of lead to the back of the driver's seat. Blood splashed the windshield.

Boris floored the van, and it rocketed away. He wove around other cars, quickly swinging back into the right lane to make the interchange. The sharp clover-leaf turn caused the suspension to squeal but the van held, and soon they were heading east in more traffic, and quickly took the first exit they came to.

Siyana jammed the Uzi back under the seat as Boris slowed for the street traffic.

Zubarev saw the Uzi too late.

He yelled something as Valeriya screamed and bullets started punching through the back of the car. Val's scream stopped short, and Zubarev snapped his eyes to her. The side of her face was gone—torn away, pieces of her on the dash and upholstery. Her blood had splashed him, he realized, as he absently looked forward again, and then the bullets ripped into his back, the stabbing pain sending electric bolts through his entire body. His hands slipped from the wheel as his vision faded and the car jolted as it left the road, heading for a cluster of trees on the shoulder. The front end caved on impact with a crunch of metal and shattering glass.

CHAPTER 2

Moscow

THE BUZZING FINALLY STIRRED Anastasia Dubinina from sleep.

She groggily reached for the phone on her nightstand and pressed a button, and the vibration stopped. She tapped in her passcode, and the screen lit up. A text message, short and frightening.

Zubarevs killed in New York. Wait for orders.

Anastasia hopped out of bed in a panic. She paced the floor of the dark room, letting out a sharp gasp, suddenly petrified by the open window before her. It let in the night air to keep the room cool, and she'd left the drapes half-open as well. She hurried around the other side of the bed and dropped to the floor. Her window was almost level with the roof of the building across the street. Was there a sniper waiting for her there?

She held the phone close, her thin nightgown bunched up around her waist.

She finally slowed her breathing and gathered her wits. This was an emergency of epic proportions; she couldn't simply "wait for orders." She dialed a number and kept her head below the top of the bed as she pressed the cell phone to her head.

Vladimir Glinkov answered right away. Glinkov was a major in the SVR, which had replaced the KGB after the fall of Communism. He, like her, was one of the leaders of the group plotting the coup.

"Are you okay?"

Her voice shook. "I'm hiding on the floor of my bedroom. I don't want to go near the window. What do we do?"

"I've been checking on everybody. So far the FSB hasn't knocked down any doors. If this was the start of a mass arrest, we'd be in prison now."

"Or worse."

"This is no time to panic. Get out if you have to, but the safehouses might be compromised."

Anastasia's hand started to shake.

"I'll wait here, I think. I don't know." She let out a string of curses.

"We'll know more in an hour. Can you hold out that long?"

"Yes."

"Call back if you don't hear from me."

Glinkov ended the call, and Anastasia set the phone down. She crawled around the bed to the nightstand, opened the drawer, and took out her Makarov pistol. She was an agent with the FSB, Russia's internal security service, and she ran through a stream-of-conscious thought process about how she was behaving like a rookie who had never been tested in battle.

But it was one thing to know you might be arrested and tried for treason. It was another thing entirely to know you *would* be arrested and tried for treason. Her hand still shook as she brought the gun back to the other side of the bed, but if anybody came through her door, people she worked with or anybody else, she'd take one or two with her before either falling to their bullets or turning the gun on herself.

Brussels, Belgium

THE LATE HOUR meant little to no traffic, and Scott Stiletto drove his rental slightly above the speed limit. Time was short, with somebody's life at stake.

Stiletto was in Brussels to collect Aliya Mussa, an ISIS operative working in Belgium. Jihadist activity had been growing in the city, beginning with the coordinated strikes against the Brussels airport and the Maalbeek metro station in March of 2016. From that point, the CIA wanted somebody on the inside. Aliya had been deeply involved in both attacks. Problem was, Aliya had a conscience, and while she had eagerly signed up for the war against the infidels, over time, she had found he could not shake the idea that what they were doing was wrong. She began feeding the CIA information about European ISIS operations, allowing the Agency and law enforcement to round up or wipe out terrorist cells before they struck again. But the enemy had discovered her, and she needed to be brought in from the cold.

He was supposed to pick her up at her apartment and take her to the rendezvous off Place des Armateurs, the rippling water of the Brussels-

Scheldt Maritime Canal providing the exit route. A speed boat waited there, the agent at the wheel ready to go full throttle once Stiletto boarded with his informant.

Stiletto, who had recruited Aliya, had drawn the assignment and developed the extraction plan. It might have seemed complicated, but ISIS had the country well-penetrated, so they needed to avoid airports and trains.

Almost there.

He slowed approaching an intersection, scanning left and right, and drove through, ignoring the traffic light.

Every minute counted.

Aliya Mussa knew she was a marked woman when an unexpected visitor knocked on the door.

Her visitor wrapped knuckles on the door three times.

A peek through the spy hole at least showed a familiar face, a man named Naadir, and as she collected a 9mm Glock from the pocket of a long coat hanging beside the door, she reflected that bad apples were always killed by people they knew.

She'd hoped the CIA would get her out before her killers showed up.

But she wasn't dead yet.

Aliya opened the door a little.

"Naadir?"

"Sorry to show unannounced, but it's important."

"What is it?"

He lowered his voice. "I'll tell you inside. There are people down the hall."

Aliya hesitated. Naadir Mohammed was a ruthless killer, the kind that liked to torture his victims as long as time allowed. He particularly liked mutilating the genitals of his victims.

"Just one second," Naadir said.

Aliya let him in. She turned her body as he entered so her back was to the door. She pushed the door shut and left the lock open.

She was dressed for running. If she had to. Jeans, T-shirt, tennis shoes. Her right hand remained behind her back.

"What is so—"

Naadir kicked her in the stomach.

Breath left her in a rush and pain exploded through her body. She collapsed, remembering to keep her grip on the gun. Her mouth was wide open but she couldn't breathe.

"We are disappointed, Aliya."

He drew a silenced automatic at the same time she lifted the Glock. She shot him in the balls. *How appropriate.* Naadir staggered back, his face turning white as he comprehended the red wetness where his manhood had been. Before he fell she shot him in the head. A spray of tissue and blood spread across the furniture behind him. When he fell, two pools of blood began soaking the carpet under him.

Aliya dropped the pistol and rose to hands and knees, gasping into the carpet now, her breathing slowly returning to normal but her midsection still hurting.

She forced herself up, leaning on the door for a moment. *Backpack, coat, now!*

Aliya ran to the hall closet where she hauled out a heavy backpack containing her "bug out" gear. Ammo, money, passport, change of clothes. Put on the long coat and scooped the Glock back into the pocket.

There are people down the hall.

Naadir hadn't been lying. Aliya spotted the back-up team, two dark-haired men, as she left the apartment. They started running toward her from the right, having been waiting near the elevator and stairwell. She raised the Glock and fired twice, turning and running for the second stairwell at the far end, which seemed a million miles away. Her shoes pounded on the hallway carpet.

The men behind her began shouting. She quickly glanced back. Neither had fallen to her salvo.

Aliya reached the stairwell door and crashed through, hurrying down two flights before stopping. Braced against the wall, she waited for the two remaining killers. When they slammed through, she worked the Glock's trigger until the gun locked open over the empty magazine.

The pistol shots echoed loudly in the contained stairwell, but Aliya paid no mind to the assault on her eardrums. Her focus was the front sight of the pistol, and making sure it lined up on the two men as they stood framed in the doorway. The 9mm stingers did their job, tearing through clothing and flesh, punching through the bodies, both men falling onto the landing, one tumbling down the steps.

With the sharp scent of cordite hanging in the air, Aliya breathlessly reloaded the pistol, snapped the slide closed, and hustled down the remaining steps.

Pushing through a doorway to the street, she paused a moment. The cool night air dried the sweat on her skin.

A car approached. She braced in the doorway. The car stopped at the curb, a man climbing out. He held a gun, but the overhead streetlamps helped her see his face. He was white. An American.

"Aliya?"

"Scott?"

"Flash," he said.

"Thunder," she replied. She left the doorway and ran to the car. He was sliding behind the steering wheel as her right hand grabbed the door handle, and then there was a burst of automatic weapons fire, and part of her right arm disappeared as the bullets cut through. A burning sensation flashed through her body. She began to fall, the back of her head striking the edge of the curb. She stayed conscious long enough to hear more shooting.

It will be okay. Stiletto is here.

Her vision faded.

· · ·

STILETTO BUMPED open the driver's door, as the fusillade of gunfire racked the passenger side of his rental, smacking the metal body and shattering windows. Aliya dropped with multiple hits, wounds that he didn't think she could survive, but he had no plans to die with her.

Stiletto rolled onto the pavement, grabbing for the .45 under his left arm. The shooter was alone, running toward them, his submachine gun in both hands. Stiletto crawled to the back end of the rental, staying low. He braced his two-hand grip on the bumper. The shooter sprayed him with a burst, but the rounds ricocheted off the pavement behind him. Stiletto's trigger pull was slow and precise, the hammer falling against the firing pin and sending a 230-grain hollow-point straight into the shooter's left hip. The bullet smashed through bones and brought the shooter down, the submachine gun slipping from his grasp to skid into the street. Stiletto jumped up, took aim again, and fired a kill shot. The shooter remained still.

Scott raced around to look at Aliya, but there was nothing he could do. If the bullets hadn't killed her, her head striking the edge of the curb finished her off.

Stiletto put his gun away and ran back to the

driver's side. He sped away with the tires screeching, his lips a tight line, jaw set. Whatever information Aliya had, it was gone, along with her, and Stiletto considered the latter a much bigger loss. She'd been a good spy.

Stiletto drove hard to the rendezvous point, screeching to a halt at the bridge on Place des Armateurs. The canal ran beneath. Stiletto left the car, running quickly down the sloping shoulder of the roadway to where the speed boat waited. He and the boat pilot exchanged the proper passwords, and the rear motor of the boat chugged to life.

Stiletto sat behind the pilot and kept his face forward. He hated leaving somebody behind. He'd lost informants before, but they were always personal losses because when you recruited somebody to spy for you, you had to meet them on an emotional level very few others could reach. One had to try to remain detached, but in Stiletto's experience, that wasn't always possible.

Aliya had been eager to do right, and paid the cost. She'd never know how much she'd contributed in the fight against terrorism. Those who put their lives on the line deserved to know the results of their risk, their sacrifice. But they often did not live long enough to do so. The lucky ones achieved the goal.

The speedboat jostled over the water, the bridge fading in the distance. They rushed past more of the city on either side, but the view did not hold his interest. He stood and moved up the narrow deck to the seat beside the driver, falling heavily into it.

"Are you hit?" the driver asked.

"I'm fine. We lost our package."

The driver said nothing and held his course.

Stiletto stared forward. He felt numb. If only he'd been a few minutes early...

Playing the "what if" game would only make the failure bigger than it was. Stiletto knew the drill. Get back to HQ, file a report, and carry on. *This is the spy business.*

But he didn't have to like it.

It wasn't a short boat ride by any means.

The canal wound 28 kilometers through Brussels and Antwerp before cutting east toward the North Sea. When the boat reached the rendezvous point about two hours later, the driver eased back on the throttle and the boat chugged along as the ocean waves rocked it up and down and back and forth. The clear early morning sky was gorgeous and, for a moment, it brought Stiletto out of his reverie.

The crash of sound about forty yards away snapped his attention away from the sky. The angled sailplanes, like wings on top of the dorsal sail, broke through the surface first, followed by the rest of the upper portion of the submarine's body. It looked like a long black sausage and created a 360-degree shockwave that hit the speedboat very quickly. Stiletto and the driver held tight as they went up and down over the crests. A crewman lowered a ladder over the side. The speedboat moved closer to the submarine with the engine burbling at near idle. Stiletto stepped off the speedboat and climbed the ladder onto the deck. He waved at the speedboat driver, who quickly powered away.

"Welcome aboard, sir," the chief petty officer said—a slim blonde man about Stiletto's age. "We were expecting a second person as well."

"So was I," Scott said as the salty wind whipped his face. "I need to get below."

"Follow me."

. . .

Stiletto shut the door of the private communications booth and called his boss at CIA headquarters via Skype. He wasn't exactly sure where the booth was located on the boat. The CPO had led him through the Byzantine maze that made up the inside of the submarine to the booth and now waited outside.

Stiletto worked for General Ike Fleming, who ran the Special Activities Division of the CIA. He was one of the better "skull smashers," as they called themselves, the agents directly responsible for the covert missions and the wet work, and whatever other dirty jobs came along. Stiletto didn't hide his grimace as his boss's face appeared on the display.

"I don't like the look on your face, Scott."

"I failed, sir."

Stiletto explained what had happened.

The general nodded sympathetically. "You know what I think, Scott."

"You think I get too close to these people."

"Besides that. You did the best you could."

Stiletto clenched his fist. Had it really been his best? But he kept the thought to himself.

"Whatever other information Aliya had," Stiletto said, "died with her."

"That's not for us to worry about right now. Get home, and we'll talk further. We'll have another opportunity."

"See you in a few days, sir."

"Try not to get seasick."

Stiletto scoffed. He hated boats for that very reason. "Last thing I need," he said, and clicked off the machine. These chats with Fleming always made him feel like he was talking to his father, the Army vet whose constant moves from base to base had left Stiletto with a problem making friends as a child. He was still learning how to do it as an adult, and maybe that was why he became too close to his recruits. Made more than the usual promises. Showed up at the first sign of an SOS.

He stared at his reflection in the blank screen for a few minutes. His face had a few character marks, but he still looked younger than his forty years, or so he thought. He needed a shave, though. Stiletto rose from the small chair and found his way out. He wanted to find a cup of tea and something to eat. He would try not to second-guess what had happened on Place des Armateurs, a street he would forever associate with failure.

. . .

STILETTO SAT at a steel table in the galley, making circles with his paper cup. The tea was half gone, and a trail of steam rose from the center.

The turkey sandwich and the tea had been good, so he felt refreshed, but he was still bothered. He had to tell himself again and again that what had occurred was part of the spy business. Wouldn't be the first or last time such a situation happened to him or any other agent.

Pots and pans clanged in the kitchen, and the voices of the head chef and his cooks provided a running soundtrack to the consumption in the galley as sailors moved in and out, taking their meals in shifts while Stiletto remained a fixed point. Luckily, they had a widescreen television playing cached recordings. As he sat, Scott watched a newsfeed that was already twenty-four-hours old.

There was no sound, but he read the closed-captioning to get the drift of what was happening.

Presently a story caught his attention and forced other thoughts away. A redheaded anchor-woman with sky-blue eyes read a story about Ravil Zubarev and his wife dying in a car crash after being fired on by another vehicle some-where in New York City. They showed photographs of the couple and a picture of the wreck.

The Zubarev name meant nothing to Scott, but as the story described Zubarev's role in Moscow politics, he couldn't help but become suspicious. Why was he in the US raising funds? Had the Kremlin machine found a way to kill him and his wife? If so, what for?

There had been a time when neither Stiletto nor anybody else in the intelligence community would have wondered if this had been a hit, but Putin's hatred for those he considered treasonous was well-known. The man was on record as saying one had to have enemies. Enemies could live as long as they were kept at bay, but traitors could not live. They had to be made an example of. Putin had made such an example of Alexander Litvinenko.

Litvinenko, a former FSB agent, had been part of an operation to take on organized crime figures throughout Russia. The task had proved nearly impossible since the Mafia clans' connections to powerful people in the government assured their protection. Later, Litvinenko accused his government of participating in the attempted assassination of a Russian oligarch named Berezovsky, whom Putin had wanted snuffed from existence for a long time for reasons that would fill three seasons of a soap opera. (Berezovsky, long after Litvinenko's own death, was found dead of an apparent suicide.)

The charges made Litvinenko *persona non grata* and he fled to London, where he became a British citizen, consulted with British intelligence, and started writing books. His books alleged that Putin had organized bombings and other terrorist acts to keep him in power, ordered the murder of a journalist named Anna Politkovskaya who had threatened to expose evidence of those crimes, and also had a working relationship with the Russian mob, using them to do his dirty work while he portrayed himself as a powerful and righteous figure on the world stage.

Such words Putin could not abide.

Litvinenko was poisoned by what was revealed to be radioactive polonium-210, and later died in November 2006.

The critic—the traitor—had been silenced.

And now Zubarev. Had the man done something to earn Putin's wrath? And had local Russian mob contacts carried out the killing? Stiletto knew from various reports which passed through his office that the Russian mob was a growing threat to US law enforcement, especially on the coasts, New York and California being their preferred stomping grounds. They were not opposed to doing Putin's bidding anywhere in the world, so they were the perfect proxy. Their orders could not be traced back to the Kremlin.

Of course, as an operative of the CIA's Special Activities Division, it wasn't any of Stiletto's business. Not yet, and probably not ever, unless a case came up outside the US where the Russkie mob threatened US security. The FBI would take charge of the homicide investigation and see where the evidence took them. Stiletto was probably being paranoid, but as a child of the Cold War, albeit the end of it, he was always suspicious of the Russians. It was his opinion that Putin wanted nothing less than to rebuild the former Soviet Union and restore his country to the superpower it had once been by any means necessary.

He had no real faith that the FBI could bring the case to Putin's door if it even went that far. When the British had investigated Litvinenko's death, they had pointed to a Russian operative named Andrey Lugovoy and accused him of the killing. Lugovoy had remained in Russia despite the UK's extradition request, but after so many years, and many leadership changes in Britain's government, they had ceased efforts to bring Lugovoy to trial. It wasn't worth the diplomatic nightmare to keep bringing up the subject.

The same would probably happen in the Zubarev case unless it was strictly a local matter.

Stiletto didn't buy that for a second.

He took a deep breath and finished what remained of his now-cold tea. The kinds of shenanigans perpetrated by Putin made him angry. Authoritarianism of *any* kind made him angry. The suppression of those who only wanted to speak out against the men in power wasn't something *he* could abide, and he fought it at every opportunity. They were the people he felt he was speaking for: the forgotten victims, the powerless, and those without a champion.

It was an endless and thankless fight, but somebody had to do it.

Stiletto tossed his cup into the trash and left the galley.

CHAPTER 3

New York City

FBI Special Agent Susan Larochelle wasn't used to coming in at nine a.m. She was normally part of the noon-to-nine crew that worked out of the New York City office, but the boss had called an emergency meeting so there she was, coffee in hand, and a *vente* at that. She was giving up her morning gym visit for this, which annoyed her. She liked order and routine, and most of the time her job at the Bureau provided exactly that. The FBI as an institution excelled at order and routine, and following such protocols had helped Susan not only rise in the ranks but become a highly-decorated investigator. Her cases had a ninety-eight percent conviction rate.

The elevator doors opened and she stepped into the noisy bullpen, then followed the walkway around the rows of desks that were perfectly aligned via Bureau guidelines. The agents at those desks were on the phone or face-down in paperwork. Up a short flight of steps to a glass-enclosed office and she said hello to her boss. All the basics were there. Blotter (clean but scuffed at the corners), computer monitor, pen set, picture of the wife. The wide window behind the chief looked out at the gray building across the street.

Jim Brody was a textbook Bureau manager: perfectly pressed Brooks Brothers suit, hair parted down the middle in a straight line, clean-shaven. He was completely useless as a field agent, but he was a good team leader, and aside from the usual "always on your ass" complaints from the agents in the bullpen, he was liked very much.

Susan sat down without invitation and Brody looked up from his paperwork. "Good morning."

"I'm not quite awake yet, chief." She sipped her coffee.

The office door swung open again, and Susan's partner Ray Elston dropped into the chair beside her. Both agents waited for Brody while the noise from the bullpen filtered through the gaps in the glass wall. It was hardly the place for a private conversation. Susan sipped her coffee again, loudly this time. Brody gave her a look as he dropped a folder in front of him and raised the flap.

"Got a dead Russian politician and his wife." Brody passed photos to Susan and Ray. "We need to know what happened."

"Saw this on the news," Ray stated. "Somebody in another vehicle shot them." He had darker hair than Brody and a Sears suit, but he had been a cop before joining the Bureau and Susan appreciated his experience.

"You know what I mean, Ray," Brody replied. "State Department wants a full report ready for when Moscow finally calls."

"Why haven't the Russians been in touch already?" Susan asked. "At least the embassy—"

"No idea, Susan. Let's have something ready for when they do. Here's the folder. Zubarev was last seen with his wife at some sort of fundraiser. Start by interviewing the guests."

Susan looked through the folder. "Their names aren't here, chief."

"I know that," Brody said. "You two are investigators. Go investigate."

Ray was out of his chair before Susan and held the door. Susan shot Brody a glare before departing.

"WHERE DO YOU WANT TO START?" Ray asked as he pulled their government-issue Ford out of the underground garage and into city traffic.

"The morgue still has the bodies and evidence from the car," Susan said, reading the notes in the folder. "Let's see what they have."

The morgue attendant had a bald head and a white beard that almost matched his white lab coat. He pulled open the cooler drawers containing the bodies of Ravil Zubarev and his wife, Valeriya. Susan shivered as the chill from the cooler drifted into the room.

The bodies were in bad shape.

The couple's skin had whitened under the chill of the cooler, ice crystals forming around their closed eyes, nostrils, and lips. Looking at the bodies, more so than the photos, made the case tangible in Susan's mind. She was solving a crime involving real people, not pictures that offered no emotional connection.

She glanced at Ray. He looked bored, but he was taking in the bodies the same as she was.

Susan nodded, and the attendant slid the cooler drawers closed. The chill went away.

"We have their belongings in the other room," the attendant said, leading them through a doorway into a smaller room with a white-tiled floor and tiled walls. A stainless-steel table sat near one of the walls, with two suitcases and a plastic bag of miscellaneous items on top. Susan and Ray started sorting through the suitcases: clothes, toiletries, a novel, the kit one packs while traveling. Nothing interesting or untoward—

"What's this?" Ray said. He lifted a metal lockbox from the suitcase of feminine clothes and set it on the table. Susan found a small gold-plated key in the bag of odds and ends and used it to open the lid. She whistled.

"The money from the fundraiser," Ray said.

A stack of cash and a stack of checks, each held together by a rubber band.

"We'll take the names from the checks," Susan said.

"I'll get the evidence bags from the car," Ray told her, and left Susan with the luggage.

Moscow

ANASTASIA DUBININA HELD her coffee cup under the table and poured in a splash of vodka from a silver flask.

She set the coffee back on the table, capped the flask, and dropped it into her purse.

"I saw that," Vlad Glinkov said as he approached the table.

Anastasia sat with her back to the wall inside the busy McDonald's. The place was full of diners, which meant it was also full of loud-enough noise to fool any electronic eavesdropping devices. She would have preferred a more comfortable chair, but no such thing was available. Everything was hard plastic, not designed for long-term sitting. The chair she sat on made her rear end sore.

Glinkov sat across from her. His back was exposed, but he showed no concern.

"Want some coffee?" she asked.

"No. What did you find out?"

"So far everybody is still on the street. No sign

of police or military anywhere. It's almost as if the murder was a message. Putin isn't rounding us up wholesale just yet."

Which, Anastasia knew, would be no easy task. Putin could kill Zubarev. He could have her and Glinkov and others arrested or killed, too. The coup plotters, however, were everywhere. Deep in the government. In the military. Putin could cut off what he thought was the head of the snake, but there were many snakes. Some of them in the Kremlin, too.

Unless...

She leaned forward. "You need to get out of Moscow."

"Soon. If they aren't watching us, there may be time. They don't know everything."

"We can't take that chance. You *do* know everything. If they make you talk—"

"I'll die first."

"You and I both know things happen so fast you might not have the chance."

"We have an opportunity to prove the conspiracy between Putin and the Mafia. We have to take the chance. If we can get world opinion on our side—"

"The world favors Putin. They'll think we're

insane. Criminals."

He put a hand on hers, but she pulled her hand back and shot him a glare.

"Ana," he soothed, "let's sit tight for now. If the worst happens, we'll deal with it."

"How?"

"We're Russians. The same way we always deal with problems."

Anastasia drank some coffee and bit off a sarcastic comeback. She'd almost forgotten her coffee. It was still warm, and the hint of vodka made it even better. She took a deep breath to calm down. A glance around the dining room revealed only couples or groups eating and engaging in animated conversation, no sign of surveillance.

Maybe Vlad was right.

"Okay," she said.

Glinkov held her eyes for a moment. "Don't drink too much."

"We're Russians," she repeated.

Glinkov frowned, rose from the chair, and left her there. She watched him exit. Nobody trailed Glinkov as he headed for the corner bus stop.

She drank more coffee and felt the vodka hit her belly. The warm glow made her forget her sore bottom.

. . .

GLINKOV FOUND a seat on the bus near the driver. Other passengers crowded the remaining seats, and the engine noise almost drowned his thoughts. The bus jostled violently over the city's rough streets.

The need to remove Vladimir Putin from office had become apparent after the nation-wide protests of 2011 through 2013, where tens of thousands had marched in Moscow, St. Petersburg, and elsewhere to challenge what many believed had been fraudulent elections where Putin cheated his way to victory. Charges of corruption and the suppression of opposing parties were also voiced by the protestors. In the end, they achieved very little. The government clamped down on organized protests, with stiff penalties for unauthorized gatherings. The Putin machine would not be moved.

A quiet whisper began drifting through opposition party leaders, the rich oligarchs who were losing money in the stagnant economy, military personnel, and people like Glinkov and Anastasia, saying that something permanent had to be done. They could not allow Putin to hijack the Presidency and leave the nation a democracy in name only.

Their first indication that Putin was feeling some kind of heat was the reduction in his inner circle. He went from having dozens of confidants and advisors to a much smaller group, all of them hard-liners who shared his vision of authoritarian rule.

The second indication was Zubarev's assassination.

The bus made a left turn, bouncing some more on the rough street. Glinkov stared at the floor.

Somehow, they had been infiltrated. They weren't ready to meet force with force, nor were they equipped to do so. Perhaps Zubarev had only been a warning, but he didn't believe that any more than Anastasia did.

The bus started for the suburbs, the road smoothing out a little. Glinkov looked up. Many of the passengers had disembarked while he was lost in thought, and of the remaining people, none appeared to notice him. His wife had their car to get their daughter back and forth to school. His routine was not hard to discern should anybody follow him.

He got the idea to send a note to the Americans to tell him what was going on. There was no way the CIA would contribute to their effort, but an official inquiry to see about a rumored connection between the Zubarev murder and the Kremlin might slow down Putin's machine.

Glinkov had worked with Scott Stiletto several times, including a mission in Russia to take out a group of neo-Nazis. Glinkov had even passed along information he thought important to the US from time to time. Had that earned him any credit with the Agency? Could he ask for asylum? Claim political persecution?

Glinkov shook his head. He could not turn his back on the Motherland, not even to protect his family. What would the others do? They didn't have the connections he had, and the US would reject him anyway. Technically, what he was doing was illegal, so a claim of persecution would fall on deaf ears.

Presently the bus reached his stop, near a park two blocks from his home, and he walked the rest of the way, senses tuned to everything around him.

Street to his left, quiet. Park to his right. People walking pets. Kids playing. Parents watching their kids and looking around. Some noticed him, but gave him no more attention than a parent taking a quick look for potential problems normally would.

Glinkov's shoes tapped a rhythm on the

concrete sidewalk. The buildings around him were gray or white and drab all over. Some things in Russia never changed. The apartments were crammed close together, having balconies on the upper floors only and mostly-empty parking lots. Glinkov's building appeared as he rounded a corner. He was lucky enough to have an upper floor, and he could see that his wife had hung out some towels on the balcony rail. Two pink towels.

Glinkov stopped and looked up and down the street. The two pink towels were a warning that somebody was watching the building, but he saw no sign of surveillance. He kept walking, and a quick glance back at the park showed nobody watching or following. The kids continued playing and making kid noises, but Glinkov couldn't hear them over the pounding of his pulse.

He cut across the street, slipping through the parking lot of the neighboring building. He used cars for cover, squatting behind an old van to check the road ahead. A few vehicles were parked on the street, but nothing that looked like an official FSB car. Then he realized the FSB wouldn't be the ones coming for him.

He glanced at the balcony of his apartment, where the towels flapped in the light breeze.

Glinkov swallowed and left the parking lot, walking briskly along the sidewalk. His pulse still hammered, but he still saw no visible threat. He cut through the hedgerow surrounding his building, following a grassy slope down to the blacktop of the parking lot and then slicing across to a narrow walkway leading to the center courtyard. He recognized a few other residents and reached the nearest elevator, pressing the button for the twelfth floor. The elevator rumbled loudly as it ascended, then the doors slid open and revealed the stained white wall and frayed yellow carpeting of his hallway.

He turned left and reached the brown door to his apartment, used his key in the lock, and pushed the door shut behind him.

"Vlad?"

He snapped his head around. Rina, his wife, stood in the entryway, her face white.

Glinkov rushed to her, hugging her close. "Why the towels?"

She squeezed him back. "They were out there earlier. Two men in a van!"

"Daddy?"

Glinkov split from his wife and scooped up his six-year-old daughter Xenia, hugging her close. She hugged back as much as her little arms allowed, then he set her down.

"When were they out there?"

"When we got home," Rina replied.

"Show me."

They moved from the entry to the living room, which was spotless, the furniture and wall fixtures old but functional. The television on the wall across from the brown couch was off. Out on the balcony, Rina pointed to a spot along the curb across the street, but there was no vehicle there now.

"I didn't see them leave," she told him.

"Okay."

They went back inside, where Xenia was watching them with wide eyes. "Mommy, what's happening?"

"It's okay, sweetie," she said, scooping her daughter up. "I have dinner in the oven."

"I need a few minutes on the computer," Glinkov told his wife. Rina took Xenia into the kitchen while Glinkov crossed the room to the corner desk where his old laptop sat. He booted up the machine and quickly accessed the internet, waiting while the connection linked to the web. He heard Rina and Xenia in the kitchen spooning food onto plates, Xenia chattering, and when he heard a spoon clatter and Xenia say, "Uh-oh," he didn't turn around. He quickly typed an email to Stiletto, his fingers flying across the keyboard. He kept the message as short and to the point as he could. When he clicked Send, he stared at the monitor for a moment. He didn't feel any better, but at least somebody on the outside would know what was going on.

"Vlad?" Rina called.

He turned in his chair.

"Your dinner's getting cold."

The front door crashed open.

His name was Rostov, and he'd have preferred to grab the woman and the child too, but orders were orders.

It hadn't been hard to figure out why the wife had hung out the towels, so he had told his support team in the van to relocate around the block. Parking in such easy view of the Glinkovs' balcony might not have been the smartest move, but the van's disappearance would throw the family off-guard long enough to get sloppy.

Rostov was a big man with a crew cut and a

graying goatee, and he was a member of the Solnt-sevskaya Bratva crime family—a senior enforcer. He had no problem doing Putin's dirty work because the cash bonuses in American dollars were funding his retirement. Another five or six years, and he'd be spending the rest of his days on the French Riviera. He already spoke the language fluently.

Rostov sat in a BMW sedan parked around the farthest end of the park from the Glinkov's apartment and used a sighting scope to observe the balcony. He watched Glinkov and his wife speak frantically, then go back inside. From what he knew of Glinkov's routine and the time of day, they'd be sitting down to dinner.

He put away the scope and pulled a cell phone from the inside pocket of his coat, then dialed the backup team leader and told them to move in. He started the car and drove into the parking lot, and the van pulled in behind him.

Rostov led the team of three into the elevator, and the machinery groaned and clanked as they went up. Rostov made fists with his hands. He carried no weapons, but the other three did, handguns they were under orders not to fire. They only needed to keep the woman and child quiet. Their orders were to leave the wife and child behind to stir panic in the other members of the cell.

The elevator doors opened, and they headed down the hall to the Glinkovs' door.

The door crashed open and slammed against the inside wall, Rostov holding it there as the three gunmen rushed in with their weapons out. The wife and daughter screamed, knocking dinner plates from counter to floor and spilling their food. The wife grabbed her daughter as two of Rostov's men held guns in their faces.

Rostov and the third goon converged on Glinkov, who stood in the center of the living room. Rostov drew a syringe from another pocket and pulled the cap off the needle.

"Traitor," Rostov accused, then ordered, "Come quietly."

"No!"

Glinkov lashed out at the nearest target, the goon with the gun, using his left hand to deflect the hand holding the pistol and his right to deliver a two-finger strike to the goon's throat. The gunman let out a strangled cry, but not before countering with a blow to Glinkov's right knee. Glinkov started to fall, taking the goon with him, and Rostov moved in with the needle. He stabbed the syringe into Glinkov's left arm, piercing cloth and skin, and pressed the plunger. By the time Glinkov and the goon hit the carpet, Glinkov was limp and out cold, and Rostov picked him up like a sack of potatoes and threw him over his shoulder.

He barked an order and started for the door. Glinkov's wife was yelling, her face streaked with tears. The little girl crying too, and Rostov had a moment of regret. It was too bad the girl would never see her father again, but that was what happened when you betrayed your country. Really, it was her father's fault.

One of the gunmen pulled the apartment door closed behind him.

CHAPTER 4

ANASTASIA HAD her gun out as soon as she heard the van's engine rev.

She was walking along Kozhukhovskaya a block away from her building, her senses overpowered by a construction crew that had one lane of the roadway closed and was using a jackhammer on the pavement. She stayed close to the wall of the building beside her, which had an art gallery on the ground floor and wide support beams holding up the floors above. The white van passed the construction zone in the open left lane, and it was so obvious who was inside that Anastasia almost laughed.

She cleared the construction zone, and the

length of open curb space ahead created the perfect spot for a grab.

The Makarov pistol warmed in her hand, and as the van sped up and approached the open curb, she pivoted left, raising the gun. As the side door slid open and a man in black started to exit, she fired. The snap of the shot, drowned out by the jackhammer, nonetheless created the expected recoil, and Anastasia let her wrist rise in a perfect follow-through.

The bullet plowed through the man's head, his face registering a brief second of shock. The back of his head exploded in a spray of blood and bone and spotted the white van with red. Anastasia ran back the way she'd come before the body hit the sidewalk.

Shocked pedestrians scattered as she ran. The corner up ahead led to Saykina, where there were warehouses and car repair shops and a freeway overpass to hide any noise. The warehouses and shops would be empty at this hour. As she turned the corner onto the tree-lined street, she stole a glance back. Another man in black clothes chased after her, his own gun out and a hunter's look in his eyes.

Anastasia reached the corner as the man fired,

and a spray of shattered brick pelted her face and neck. She ignored the sting and kept going, heading toward the entrance of an alley up ahead. She turned into it but stopped short when the white van entered from the other side, its bright headlamps hitting her like a spotlight. She fired twice, and one of the headlamps winked out and the windshield spider-webbed on the passenger side. She turned to exit as the pursuing gunman entered the alley, and Anastasia put two rounds into his chest. She leaped over his falling body and ran into the middle of the street, then crossed to the sidewalk opposite and found a padlocked garage door—one of the car repair shops. The gray sheet metal door clashed with the red brick of the rest of the building. She shot off the lock, raised the door, and slipped through the opening, and the garage door slammed shut behind her. She stood in the dark for a moment, then carefully moved forward, bumping into cars on the paved floor and up on lifts. The garage door started to rise, clanging loudly. Anastasia dropped between a car and a trio of oil drums, shifting to avoid a patch of oil on the ground. The place smelled not only of motor oil but of tire rubber and stale sweat. The garage door went up some more, and she slapped a fresh magazine into the Makarov.

A pair of gunshots cracked, and the garage door slammed closed. Her ears rang with the racket and she rested her arms on the hood of the car, holding her gun in both hands. The garage door opened again and she tightened her finger on the trigger, but held her fire when she saw the face of the man holding up the door.

"Ana!"

It wasn't the man from the van, she knew that for sure. It was Dimitri Ravkin, a friend and member of the group plotting the coup.

"It's Dimitri, Ana. We gotta go!"

Anastasia let out the breath she was holding and emerged from cover to approach Ravkin. The body of the van's driver lay near him, a pool of the man's blood heading for the street.

"How did you find me?" she asked.

"They tried for me, and you were the next closest target," Ravkin explained. "We need to hurry."

She hesitated, the Makarov still in her hand, but freezing up was crazy. Ravkin was a friend and a fellow SVR agent, somebody she trusted. He stood there in his usual brown leather jacket, white t-shirt, and jeans, wiry but plenty of muscle, his jawline showing the kind of rugged sharp edge she found irresistible. The worst was happening, and they needed to close ranks and regroup. She went to Ravkin. He let the garage door drop shut and they ran to his car, which he'd left running in the alley next to the shop. She piled into the passenger seat, and Ravkin accelerated to the street ahead.

"Where are we going?" she asked.

"Safehouse."

"They're compromised!"

"I have my own. Nobody knows about it, not even Glinkov."

"Did they get him?"

"I think so."

Anastasia slammed a fist on the dash.

"Don't hurt my car," Ravkin requested.

"This is no time for jokes."

"Right now we need to focus. Once we get to the safehouse, we'll see where we stand."

Anastasia put away her gun and looked ahead. Ravkin made another turn and headed for the freeway. No time for jokes, indeed. She wondered if they had any time left at all.

McLean, VA – CIA Training Facility

STILETTO SAT on the ground and folded his legs, placing his automatic, holster, and shooting glasses on the ground beside him.

Shots still popped inside the single-story building ahead of him, but his drill was finished. He'd returned from overseas with orders to head for the Farm, the CIA's training center, and get started on his brush-up of basic skills. He figured it was Fleming's way of keeping him from moping around the office. Scott did find that the concentration kept his mind off other things, and day by day, he was feeling better—just in time to leave in the morning.

This particular shooting range was located in an open field, with green grass and rolling hills nearby. Other training areas were visible in the distance. It was almost a vacation. The wind blew gently, and a few birds flew by now and then. Stiletto wished he had his sketchbook to get down some of the surrounding scenery, but he made mental notes to draw as soon as he returned to the barracks.

"Finished for the day?"

Stiletto looked up as David McNeil walked toward him carrying his own shooting gear. McNeil was General Fleming's chief of staff. A covert ops veteran, he'd only taken the chief of staff job after losing his left leg during an assignment. Nobody could tell he had a prosthetic from the knee down unless he wore shorts as he did now, his leg reflecting the bright sunlight. He liked to take his refresher courses at the Farm to show up the new recruits. He'd never see a field assignment again, but being able to keep up was almost as good.

"Pretty much," Stiletto replied. "I leave tomorrow."

McNeil sat down, folding his left leg under his right, which remained outstretched with the prosthetic.

"Sorry about Belgium," McNeil remarked.

"Thanks." Stiletto stared into the distance.

"What else is on your mind?"

"Did you happen to see my report about San Francisco?"

Stiletto's last mission to the City by the Bay had been unofficial but related to a mission that began in Switzerland. An old girlfriend, Ali Lewis, who also happened to be a former Agency employee, had needed help after somebody murdered her father.

"I saw it," McNeil said. "What did you leave out?"

"Ali offered me a job."

"Doing what?"

"Drawing sketches for her clothing lines or something like that. We didn't have a lot of time to talk about it."

"Are you thinking of taking it?"

"I don't know."

McNeil didn't respond right away. The shooting continued inside the building, single shots followed by strings of rapid fire.

"You can't do this job forever, Scott."

"What does that mean?"

"You're not getting any younger, and look at me! Sometimes the worst happens even when you do everything right."

"I can't see myself doing anything else."

"You're not going to spout one of those riffs about the defenseless, are you?"

Stiletto laughed. "Hey, have a heart."

"In the end, we put our butts on the line, and nobody cares. If you have the chance to get out and settle down somewhere nice, I think you should do it. You'll be given a desk job in two years anyway, 'cause you gettin' old, buddy."

"I know, but I'm not ready to stop yet."

McNeil tapped his aluminum leg. "Neither was I."

STILETTO RETURNED HOME the next afternoon and parked his "new" car in the driveway.

He had a base-model Chevy Cruze, which was a good car but hardly a replacement for his restored '77 Trans Am, which had been shot to pieces in his driveway by an Iranian assassin firing from the cover of his porch.

He locked the car and carried his suitcases inside. On the table against the wall in front of him sat a pile of mail, dutifully collected by one of the young bucks in Scott's department who also made a daily security check of the home. Remembering his own days of such grunt work, Scott had left the youngster a six-pack of beer, and found to his delight that the fellow had left him two cans. The kid would do well indeed.

He drank the beer on the couch, with *Pawn Stars* on the television and his laptop on his lap. Perusing his email, Stiletto ignored Rick Harrison's usual dribble about needing a buddy to check this or that and hit the Delete button repeatedly until he came to a note from Vladimir Glinkov.

He muted the television and read, his pulse quickening as he hit the major points.

Zubarev murder in New York.

Planned coup to depose Putin.

Russian mafia as Putin's proxy.

Help.

Stiletto read the note twice, growing more alarmed by the second. Clicking on his Dissenter internet browser, Scott searched for more on the Zubarev killings, but found nothing to add to what he'd already learned on the submarine.

Back to his inbox. He saw a second note from Vlad, sent after the first. But this one was signed by his wife and chilled Stiletto's blood.

They came and took him.

Don't know what to do.

Stiletto connected wirelessly to the printer in his office down the hall and printed both emails, then he folded the sheets of paper into a pocket and grabbed the keys to the Chevy.

. . .

STILETTO PACED the floor while General Ike Fleming, the man in charge of the Special Activities Division, stoically read each of the printed emails.

Pictures around the office showed General Fleming in various stages of his Army career. He'd only been in charge of the Special Activities Division for three years, having joined after retiring from the military, but to his agents, it felt like he'd been there forever. He knew how to champion his people, and they wanted to do right by him because he took care of them.

No family pictures adorned the desk. Fleming kept family details private, but everybody knew he'd been married to the same woman for almost forty years.

"Stop pacing and sit down, Scott."

"I can't stay still, sir."

"Sit down so I can talk to you. Now."

Stiletto paused. Fleming set the papers down, removed his glasses, and looked up expectantly. His dark eyes repeated the order, and Stiletto took a seat in front of the general's desk.

"What am I supposed to say about this?" Fleming asked.

"They need our help, sir."

"Who needs our help? A man acting illegally to overthrow a lawfully-elected leader?"

"That's a load of crap, and you know it."

Fleming raised an eyebrow.

"Sir," Stiletto added.

The general sat back, hands over his stomach. "But how does the rest of the world see Putin? What is our official policy toward Russia? You and I and, hell, half this Agency know the truth, but there's nothing we can do."

"What about the murders and the Mafia angle? Surely that makes it our business."

"Not *this* department's business. The FBI will handle the investigation and, if necessary, the State Department will open a dialog on the other matter. I know what you want, Scott. Glinkov is a friend who has done favors for this Agency. But there's nothing we can do."

"What about unofficially?"

Fleming leaned forward, raising his voice. "You know damn well what will happen if you are caught on Russian soil trying to interfere. The diplomatic nightmare will set relations back decades. No, Scott. I know this stings after Belgium, but Glinkov knew the risks. He also had no business contacting you, I might add."

"Except for maybe asylum."

"Which wouldn't get anywhere either. Planning a coup is illegal. He can't claim persecution when the police are only doing their job and arresting somebody with violent intentions against the government. And it's been forty-eight hours. If he hasn't already been shot, he's well away from Moscow."

Stiletto clenched his jaw. "And his wife and kid?"

"I'm sorry. If it were up to me—"

"I get it, sir."

"It's the spy business."

"It's politics."

"That too."

"And it's all bullshit."

"I don't disagree," the general said. "But we have to be realistic."

The two men watched each other quietly, Stiletto feeling like a ball of energy contained in a box and ready to explode.

Fleming asked, "Anything else?"

Stiletto rose from the chair. "I guess not." He started for the door.

"Scott?"

He turned.

"Be here bright and early tomorrow."

"Yes, sir."

Stiletto exited the office.

STILETTO DROVE ALMOST IN A TRANCE. As he sat in late afternoon freeway traffic, he started outlining a plan. By the time he pulled up in the driveway, he knew what he was going to do.

The risks were high. He could lose his life and/or his job, the job he wasn't ready to leave yet. He might end up in prison on the other side of the world, or he might single-handedly create an international incident.

Part of him wanted to follow orders and leave it alone.

But at his most desperate moment, Glinkov had reached out to him for help.

Scott couldn't ignore that.

Maybe it was too late for Vlad, and if so, Scott could at least get Rina and Xenia out of Russia to someplace safe. He knew what it was like to lose his family, and he didn't want that burden on Glinkov or his wife and daughter. If there was any possibility he could rescue Glinkov and reunite him with his family, he had to try.

Stiletto locked the car and went inside, where he put the kettle on, brewed some very powerful Earl Gray, and got out a map of Moscow.

New York City

"No, I won't talk to you! Go away!"

FBI Special Agent Susan Larochelle flinched as the door slammed.

"So much for the first interview," said her partner Ray Elston.

They had made a list of interview subjects from the names on the Zubarevs' checks. The house they stood in front of wasn't the largest in the neighborhood, but it sat at the top of a hill in the gated community, with surrounding trees. The garden in the front yard seemed to be a little much. The agents couldn't take a step without bumping into another rose bush or hedgerow, and they could barely see the house from the street with all the clutter.

The curtain covering the window next to the door shifted, a face appearing behind the glass. "Go away!"

Susan stepped off the porch first and Ray

followed, a wall of rose bushes on either side of the walk.

"Who's next?" she asked as she drove away.

Elston consulted their list. Petukhov "Peter" Igorevich and his wife Galina lived in Forest Hills. A housekeeper answered the door, and Susan's FBI badge startled her, and she fetched the lady of the house.

Galina Igorevich was in her sixties and wore a blue dress with a white pearl necklace. She invited the agents inside. The opulent home had marble flooring in the entryway and a sitting room on either side. Mrs. Igorevich led them to the room on the right, and asked the housekeeper to bring coffee and tea. When the housekeeper asked where the silver was, Igorevich explained that the house-keeper was a new hire and excused herself to go and show the woman where to find the silver. Susan looked around. Thick white carpet, fancy decorations. The paintings on the walls looked expensive and also original; either that, or they were very good reproductions. She wasn't an art expert and couldn't identify any of the work, but she knew nice paintings when she saw them.

Mrs. Igorevich quickly returned, alone, and yelled for her husband.

"We've been waiting for you," Mrs. Igorevich told them. "We have a lot to say."

"You don't know why we're here," Susan replied, although she knew full well the woman did. She wanted to hear her say it.

"You're here because of the murder."

Mr. Igorevich entered. He was a little younger than his wife and had a shock of white hair. He shook hands with the agents. The housekeeper returned with coffee, tea, and a plate of cookies and she poured, lifting the teakettle with her right arm. Susan couldn't help but notice how knobby her elbow looked. The housekeeper served everyone and left the room.

Peter and Galinda Igorevich sat across from Susan and Elston, a glass coffee table between them. Susan held her coffee by the saucer and spoke to the couple.

"What happened on the night of the seventeenth?" she asked.

Mrs. Igorevich answered.

"We attended a fundraiser for the People's Freedom Party that opposes Putin." The couple talked about the meeting and what was said. Susan asked why the party had to raise money in the US and the couple became very animated, raising their voices as they lashed out at Putin and the way he ran their former home country.

"Are you suggesting that the Russian government was responsible for the murders?" Susan said.

"He did it," Mrs. Igorevich stated firmly. "I don't know how, but he did. It is shameful, and the US must do something to stop Putin, not idolize him. Too many Russians died defeating the Communists for Putin to be tolerated."

Ray Elston scribbled appropriate information and made a show of taking notes on the accusations. Susan watched his pen scratch the notepaper. His pretend notes looked like a shopping list for later in the evening. She thanked them for their time, and she and Ray took their leave. The couple, all smiles, said they were happy to help. They wanted to get the truth out.

Susan drove away as Ray looked over his notes.

"So you're out of bananas?" Susan asked.

Ray didn't laugh.

"How many more times are we going to hear a similar story?" he replied.

"How many names are left on the list?"

MR. IGOREVICH WATCHED the FBI agents drive

away as his wife gathered the cups and saucers.

The housekeeper walked toward him with a stern look on her face. She kept her right hand close to her leg to hide the pistol she carried. When Mr. Igorevich turned, she raised the gun, and he blinked in surprise before she shot him in the head. He crashed to the floor, staining the white marble red.

Mrs. Igorevich screamed and dropped the cups and saucers, which shattered on the carpet. The housekeeper shot her in the head as well, and bits of her brain and skull fragments splattered on one of the wall paintings.

Siyana Antonova lowered the gun. The Igoreviches had been identified as the most likely of the fundraiser attendees to blab to the feds, and their deaths would send a shockwave through the rest of the traitors. Nobody else would talk.

The murders were ill-timed, of course, but she wasn't worried about the agents learning about the shooting. Their investigation wouldn't get much farther, she knew.

With the stink of cordite hanging in the room, Siyana retreated to her room off the kitchen to grab her getaway kit.

Virginia

STILETTO STOPPED MAKING notes as soon as he heard crickets through the open windows.

He needed to be totally off the grid, which meant not using a computer or any electronics that could be traced.

He had backup cash stashed as well as false passports, at least three to choose from. Every field agent had cover identities prepared outside the Agency in case they ever needed to disappear. The cash had come from unused operational funds Scott had secreted away. Unethical, maybe. Well, probably. But the money was there for emergencies, and this extraction certainly qualified.

To him, anyway.

He needed transportation out of the country, and that was proving difficult. Scott couldn't use any Agency assets or individuals easily connected to him, which meant minor-league smugglers. There was one in Canada Stiletto knew about who ran goods through Eastern Europe. That would be his first stop.

Finally, he took a break, brewed more tea, and stepped out to the backyard to light a cigar, a Montecristo '93 Vintage Club Cabinet. He listened to the crickets and looked at the half-moon in the night sky.

He thought of the consequences once again, and once again dismissed them.

Scott could not sit by idly while a friend suffered for doing the right thing. He had to do the right thing too. Maybe it was a sign. Perhaps it was time to move on, or, should he survive and be fired, join Ali Lewis in San Francisco.

He took his time with the cigar, enjoying the coolness of the night. His tea went cold before he finished, and he tossed the remaining liquid into the yard.

Back inside, he fixed ham and eggs and ate standing in the kitchen, then cleaned up and went into his bedroom, where he packed a tote with clothes and other travel necessities. Scott found himself moving slowly. With each item, he was closer and closer to crossing a line he might not be able to cross back over.

He showered, then sat up in bed going over his notes one more time.

The bank opened at nine in the morning.

Scott planned to be there when they unlocked the front door.

CHAPTER 5

"HE'S LEAVING THE HOUSE," Tom Winkler said. He spoke into the com link in his ear, which resembled a normal Bluetooth unit.

"We see him," said the secondary unit.

Winkler stepped on the gas and followed Stiletto's car.

It wasn't the most ambiguous assignment Winkler had ever been given, but it was unusual to trail one of their own without at least knowing what the problem was. The order from the top was to follow Stiletto and make sure he went to work. Huh? If he didn't, Winkler had orders to intercept. At least *that* part he understood.

Morning traffic provided ample cover for him and his secondary team. He rode alone, while the other team was a pair of fellow shadowers as confused about the assignment as he was. If Stiletto did what he was supposed to do, they could call it a day.

It was about twenty to nine by Winkler's dash clock when Stiletto pulled into the parking lot of a bank. Winkler cruised by, found curbside parking half a block away, and went back on foot. Stiletto remained in his car since the bank wasn't open yet.

Into his com, Winkler said, "What's your location?"

"Opposite end of the block from you. We can see him if that tree doesn't move."

Winkler looked. The tree in question sat off Stiletto's back bumper.

"Copy. The tree should be fine." He grinned. They might not understand the job, but there was no reason not to have fun with it.

Winkler found cover behind the building next door, a cigar shop that was also still closed, and waited by a dumpster with a chain-link fence between him and the bank parking lot. Stiletto appeared not to be looking for a tail and he'd made no attempt to shake surveillance on his drive to the bank, so Winkler's mind raced with possibilities. Was this some kind of test? Or was Stiletto a dirty agent the boss was trying to catch? Winkler didn't know the man, so he had no idea of Stiletto's abilities or rank in the Agency. He was an assignment, that's all, so a brain teaser it remained.

Winkler used his cell phone to check in with the office and report his position.

THE BRANCH MANAGER unlocked the doors.

Stiletto wasn't the only one to enter right away. A man in a business suit made a beeline for the loan desk, and a soccer mom headed for the tellers. Stiletto stopped in line behind her, and it only took a second to get in front of a window. He showed his ID and ATM card asked to access his safe deposit box.

Presently the teller brought him to a small room where the safe deposit boxes lined three walls. A table sat in the center of the room. Stiletto found his box number, both he and the teller inserted their keys, and unlocked the box. The teller departed. Stiletto removed the rectangular container inside.

Lifting the lid, Stiletto began transferring items from the container to a tote bag he carried: several stacks of cash (used bills), one passport from the three in the bag, which identified him as a Canadian, a box of .45 ACP ammunition, and a burner cell phone, which he powered up and dropped into a coat pocket.

He closed the lid and let out a long breath. Wow. He was really doing this.

Stiletto returned the container to the locker and gave the key a sharp twist.

STILETTO APPROACHED his car at a brisk pace. He was in a hurry now. His scan picked up only normal activity until he saw a man in his mid-thirties walking toward him.

"Stop right there, Stiletto."

Scott froze, watching the guy as he approached. The man was holding up a hand instead of a gun.

A sedan with two occupants turned into the parking lot and blocked the driveway near Stiletto's car. The exit, a few feet away, remained unblocked.

Stiletto opened the back door of the Chevy and dropped the tote inside. He then shut the door and took two steps toward the approaching man, who stopped short and seemed a little surprised by the move.

"What is it?"

"We're here to escort you."

"Where?"

"To work."

Stiletto laughed. "That's rich. Was this the general's idea?"

"I have no idea. I have my orders."

"Stuff 'em."

Stiletto turned and reached for Chevy's door handle.

His next move wasn't exactly a reflex since he'd watched the man's reflection in the window of the car. The man moved toward him, slipping a collapsible baton out from under his sports jacket. Stiletto pivoted, snapping his right leg up and out, the high kick connecting with the man's right arm, the hand of which held the baton. The man yelled and dropped the baton, not falling over until Stiletto delivered another fast kick to his midsection.

By then the two men from the sedan were out of the car and running toward him. Stiletto snatched up the fallen baton and extended it with the snap of his wrist. The two men stopped, holding up their hands. One said, "Whoa, it's not supposed to be like this!"

"Stay back or it will get worse," Stiletto told him, opening the door and dropping behind the wheel. He started the motor. The two men from the sedan ran to their comrade and pulled him out of the way as Stiletto reversed and squealed his tires, racing for the exit.

Stiletto took deep breaths as he merged with traffic. He hadn't expected anything like that, but he could put the blame on the general's desk. Scott's hands tightened on the wheel. He didn't blame his chief, but the move still made him angry.

He didn't want what would possibly be his last thoughts of the general to be negative.

Stiletto headed for the freeway and drove north, destination Montreal and a smuggler named Hammond.

THE BANK MANAGER and a loan officer came out to see about the commotion, and Winkler asked them not to call the police. When they asked why, he showed them his ID, which identified *him* as the police, and boy, wasn't this embarrassing?

His partners helped him into the back seat of their car, and they drove away.

What was in the tote bag? Maybe that was what the fuss was about.

All Winkler knew as he sat in the back seat was that he'd have a big bruise on his arm, and his belly hurt, and he'd need a new baton. Luckily the kicks hadn't been as hard as Stiletto could have delivered them. He hadn't been trying to hurt anybody, just get away.

But why?

Moscow

It wasn't so much a safehouse as a basement.

Anastasia Dubinina paced the concrete floor as a corner television, the sound low, filled the room with a flickering glow. The news was on, and none of it was good. However, Anastasia wasn't sure how much she should believe. It *was* Russia, after all. The news anchors talked of arrests and forthcoming statements by the Kremlin, as well as a speech by Putin, live. They showed no pictures of those who had been arrested, and only spoke in generalities regarding the "alleged coup," but the words cut through her bones.

And she kept waiting for the door to open.

The basement had the common room she paced in, and down a short hallway, there was a trio of bedrooms with bunks. It was a crude setup, with electricity and running water and one cramped bathroom. It had all been shoe-horned into the space never intended for occupation more than a few days, or even hours. As Anastasia waited for the door to open, she wondered how long they'd be there.

Finally, the door did open on quiet hinges, and Dimitri Ravkin led two frightened females into the room. One was Rina Glinkov, her skin pasty-white; the other was her daughter Xenia. The little girl clutched a brown teddy bear. Of course, she would. Anastasia's heart broke.

"I thought you'd never get back," Anastasia blurted.

"Streets are crawling with Army," Ravkin reported. He pulled the door shut, locked it, and pressed two buttons on a wall panel beside the door. A monitor next to the panel flickered to life and offered a view of the alley behind the building.

Anastasia introduced herself to Mrs. Glinkov, who shook her hand weakly. Xenia was equally unresponsive, even when Anastasia complimented the teddy bear.

Ravkin showed the Glinkov women to one of the bedrooms. Anastasia prepared coffee in the small nook that served as the kitchen, which contained a microwave, the coffee maker, and two hot plates on top of a cabinet that held other necessary items.

"What's on the news?" Ravkin asked. He turned on an overhead light, which drowned out the flickering glow and made Anastasia feel almost like she was home. Maybe she should have turned them on earlier.

"Apparently we've all been arrested, and Putin will speak soon," she told him.

Ravkin found a seat on the couch to watch the news. Still, they showed no pictures of any arrests, and Ravkin pointed that out. "If they had as much as they say, they'd be showing pictures. They'd be gloating."

"Nobody's checked in yet, Dimitri, and I can't reach anyone either."

Ravkin let out a breath.

Rina slowly entered the room. "I think Xenia will sleep for a while, but I expect her to wake up through the night. Do I smell coffee?"

Anastasia rushed to serve the woman a

steaming mug, and Ravkin made room for her on the couch.

"This is all so scary," Glinkov's wife said. "The way the broke into my home—" She stifled a cry and covered her mouth.

Anastasia rubbed Rina's back. There was no point in making any false promises or offering platitudes. Glinkov was probably already dead, and they'd find out for sure soon enough if the government tracked them down and brought them to the same place. That was most likely any forest outside Moscow, where Putin's executioners carried out their murders and buried people deep enough so animals didn't dig up the bodies.

All thoughts left her mind when the symbol of the Kremlin flashed on the television.

Ravkin turned up the volume.

Putin appeared behind a podium with two of his usual advisors, who stood in front of a covered table while Putin outlined the story of the attempted coup and the rounding up of suspects. When he made a show of removing the cover from the table, he revealed explosives and weapons he claimed were found in the homes and offices of the arrested coup plotters. The camera made a slow crawl over the items, which included Semtex explosives and Kalashnikovs. Anastasia tapped her lips, her stomach in knots. Rina Glinkov watched stoically. Ravkin was pale.

Putin remarked that there were still some suspects on the run, but they would be captured soon enough, putting an end to what might have been a nightmare for the Russian people. The Kremlin symbol appeared again, and then a commercial for Nurofen Lady, featuring a woman complaining about her abdominal cramping, came on.

It was all too much for Anastasia. She lunged at the tv and turned it off.

"Impossible," Ravkin said. "Those weapons were stashed in the country. No way they got there so fast."

"Not unless Vlad talked," Anastasia shot back.

Rina gasped.

"Or," she added, "maybe they've known more about us than we realized this whole time."

The three of them looked at each other. Anastasia wondered which of them was in charge, her or Ravkin. Since he wasn't talking, she spoke up, taking the lead.

"We are no good to anybody all riled up," she

continued. "Let's get some rest and see what happens in the morning."

Ravkin raised an eyebrow. "No. One of us needs to be up at all times, and I'll take the first watch. The two of you try to rest."

Anastasia didn't argue. She and Rina went down the hall. Ten minutes later, Anastasia lay on her bunk, still dressed, and staring at the ceiling. She didn't see any way out of their predicament, but they owed it to the rest of the team to try to escape and tell the world why they had done what they did. Maybe the weapons cache had been raided, but what about the money they'd hidden? They could get passports created, adopt mild disguises, and find a way out of Russia.

It was their only hope.

Virginia

GENERAL IKE FLEMING made room on the bench for another man in a Brooks Brothers suit and offered him a bite from his box of fish and chips. The new arrival waved off the offer.

"So?" Fleming said.

Charlie Devlin of the DC office of the FBI

folded his arms. "It took some arm-twisting to get the warrant, but we checked the safe deposit box. Some cash and two passports."

"That's it?"

"Yup. Your office should have the passport information shortly."

"Won't do us any good," Fleming said, biting off a piece of fish. "Those passports will be in names not associated with Scott's file."

"He's going off-grid?"

"Precisely."

"Is it time to call our friends?"

"I think so. He'll need some help."

"Let me know if there's anything else I can do," Devlin said. Fleming wiped his hand on a napkin, shook with the G-man, and watched him walk away.

Joggers passed, and there were kids playing somewhere behind him. Fleming finished his lunch and set the box aside. Taking out his cell phone, he made a call to an international number and stayed on the line for ten minutes.

DAVID MCNEIL, Fleming's chief of staff, entered Stiletto's home using a spare key Scott had left at the office. Every agent provided the office with access to their homes in case of an emergency such as the one they faced now.

He closed the door. The alarm system was on, and McNeil punched in the deactivation code. Then he moved through the quiet house quickly and efficiently, checking the rooms first out of habit, then starting a thorough search.

There were obvious clues right away.

Clothes missing.

Stiletto's wallet and cell phone on the bedside nightstand. The wallet contained his driver's license and credit cards—the usual items. There was no cash. The cell phone had been turned off.

McNeil walked around the backyard, noticing a stray bucket in the middle of the grass right away. He went over to the bucket and examined the burned mess of paper at the bottom. He found an unburned piece and read the words on it, which confirmed what they had figured out. At least they now knew for sure.

McNeil reset the alarm and left the house.

CHAPTER 6

FLEMING ENTERED his outer office where McNeil sat. The two men acknowledged each other, and McNeil followed Fleming into the inner office. While the general hung up his coat beside the door, McNeil started his report.

"I found a bucket in the backyard with the burned remains of a map," McNeil stated.

Fleming moved behind his desk and told McNeil to sit as well, which he did.

"Do I need to guess?"

"Moscow, sir."

"Go on."

"Wallet and cell phone remained on his dresser."

"He won't be traveling under his own name."

Fleming recounted what Devlin had discovered at the bank.

"How are we supposed to track him, then?" McNeil said. "There's been nothing from the facial recognition equipment at the airports, so we have to assume he's on the road. He's been gone for hours, which means he could be anywhere."

Fleming nodded.

"And he'll have changed cars. Tracking his license plate won't help."

"We need to do that anyway, just because."

"Who can he reach out to?" McNeil asked.

"He won't use anybody obvious or connected to us, so here's what we do: send word to every nook and cranny, every two-bit shady operative, friend and foe, that there's a one-million-dollar reward out for information leading to Scott's location."

McNeil stared.

"I'm not kidding, David. If that's what it takes to find him, I'll take the money from our operating budget and deal with the consequences later. What we can't have is Stiletto causing trouble in Russia."

"Okay, sir."

"This isn't the usual routine, David, I realize that. We have to be flexible."

"You've said it before, sir. It's the spy business." McNeil rose from his chair. "I'll get back to you if something comes in."

Fleming nodded and sat back in his chair as McNeil pulled the door shut behind him. The general sat still and thought about the phone call he'd made from the park. There had been no other choice. Scott was too good an operative not to have a plan for avoiding detection. They needed help that was as off-the-grid as he now was. Fleming hoped Scott would recognize the help when it arrived, because one way or another, Stiletto's life was going to change over the next few days.

Fleming didn't consider himself reversing from what he had told Scott. The Agency could not in any way, shape, or form take part in getting Glinkov and his family out of Russia.

But that didn't mean a separate group made up of intelligence professionals acting on their own couldn't help.

Fleming belonged to such a group. On the side, of course.

A group that called itself The Trust. He had to make sure they found Scott before the CIA did.

New York City

FBI SPECIAL AGENT Susan Larochelle wasn't feeling very special as she locked the door of her apartment.

It was almost ten p.m., and it had been another day of fruitless interviews with Russians who refused to talk, especially after the murders of Mr. and Mrs. Igorevich started filtering through the news. Two other agents had been assigned to look into the murders while she and Ray continued with their interviews. The people were scared. They did not want to talk, no matter what verbal persuasions she and Ray tried.

Somebody wanted the investigation stopped, and was going about it perfectly.

She set her purse down on the kitchen counter and went into the bedroom to change from suit to sweats. She was in no mood to cook, so she made a sandwich and ate in the kitchen. Then she poured a glass of red wine and dropped onto the couch with the tv on low.

A channel had *Law & Order* on; she considered that a comedy. She ignored the news. Finally, she settled on a *Match Game '73* rerun on the Game Show Network. Seventies-era outfits and jokes were a lot more palatable than the other dreck.

She finished the glass of wine and poured another, then opened the drapes, which revealed her balcony. She opened the sliding glass door a crack to let some air in.

And then the glass shattered.

As the pieces pooled around her feet and the wine stained the rug, the bullet that crashed through reached the opposite end of the room and shredded the door of a cabinet. Susan dropped and hurriedly crawled around the side of the couch as cold air rushed in. Some remaining pieces of glass in the door frame dropped on the carpet. She glanced down at her feet; small cuts on both, nothing terrible. Her heart pounding, she waited. And waited some more.

The phone rang.

She looked over her shoulder at the wall-mounted landline. She hardly remembered it existed sometimes, but there it was, ringing and ringing. She crawled around the dining table behind her, rose as high as she dared, and reached for the phone, returning with the handset to her low position on the carpet.

"Hello?" she answered. The instinct that had made her answer was confirmed when the person on the other end, a female, spoke.

"Stop your meddling or the next one goes through your head."

The caller hung up.

Someone pounded on the door.

"Susan! Susan, it's Ray! *Open up!*"

She ran to the door and yanked it open. "Oh, my God, Ray!"

A trickle of blood was working its way down Ray's face and neck, but he appeared unharmed otherwise. Susan pulled him in and shut the door.

"What happened?"

"Shooter on the roof near my place. Got me as I was climbing the steps."

"Look over there."

"I wondered why it was so cold in here."

"The shooter called. Told us to knock it off or she won't miss next time."

Ray Elston took a deep breath, then his eyes widened and his stance wavered. He leaned against the wall. "I think I need to lie down somewhere."

Susan grabbed flip-flops from the bedroom and her purse from the kitchen. "Not here. Let's get you to a hospital."

The ER rushed Ray into an exam room while Susan remained in the waiting room. She paced a lot, sitting for short spells while ignoring the wide-screen tv on the wall and the late-night talk shows it was showing. A perusal of the usual magazines also couldn't calm her nerves.

Around one a.m., her boss finally returned the two frantic calls she'd made to him.

"Where are you?" Jim Brody asked.

"ER," she said. "Ray got a graze." She told him what had happened at her apartment.

"Russian caller, you say?"

"Female. The bullet parted my hair, Jim."

"I'll send a team to your place, Ray's too. Get them secured and your window fixed. You two need to hole up for a bit."

The FBI maintained a pair of hotel rooms downtown for agents, witnesses, and special guests to use, and the rooms were currently empty. Brody told Susan to go there.

"That treats the symptoms," Susan said, "but it doesn't solve the problem."

"We'll work on the problem, but right now I

need you two safe. Get some rest, and don't come in till late afternoon."

After Ray exited the examining room with the side of his face appropriately stitched and bandaged, she drove them to the hotel. Neither had a change of clothes, but they gathered other necessities at the hotel gift shop. They'd deal with the other problem later.

Susan was brushing her teeth with the too-small travel brush and not her preferred brand of toothpaste when her cell phone rang. She didn't recognize the number, but she spat and rinsed and then answered.

"This is Susan."

A heavily accented voice came over the line— another Russian, this time a male.

"We spoke earlier today."

"I talked to a lot of people today. What's your name?"

"I am Yuri Olinov."

Susan didn't specifically remember the man. She wished she had her notes with her, but she'd obviously given him her cell number.

"What can I do for you, Yuri?"

"I have information I want to give you. They are watching us. If they had seen me hand it to you,

I would have been killed. I have put it in the mail. You should receive it soon."

"What kind of information?"

"Answers to your questions and more. I have to go."

Susan tried to respond, but the line went dead. She put the phone down and stared at her feet, which were still spotted with blood. She hadn't bothered to clean up. A quick shower changed that, and she dropped into bed naked. She tried to ponder the new development, but sleep quickly overtook her.

THE FIRST THING Stiletto did after leaving the bank was ditch his car.

He left it on a street in downtown Manassas and walked to an Enterprise office, where they fixed up him with another vehicle under the name on his new ID. He was traveling as Peter Drumm. He couldn't remain in his Chevy because there'd be an all-points bulletin out for it. Before leaving Manassas, he purchased hair dye and some other miscellaneous items, and then he headed north on his twelve-hour drive to Montreal.

He followed East 66 to start, heading through

Delaware toward New York. He stopped at a few rest areas along the way, with a New York State Trooper making him a little nervous for a particular stretch. The officer made no move to pull him over, though. Stiletto had already made up his mind that should such a thing happen, he'd surrender. There was no point in putting up a fight with local authorities.

He pushed on toward Albany and started getting hungry, so he found a Denny's and ate dinner. Then he decided to call it a night and found a Motel 6 off I-90. There would be facial recognition cameras at the border, so he went about planning his disguise before bed. Change of hair color, glasses, beard. His five o'clock shadow was already showing, and by the time he reached Canada, it would have grown in a little more. He'd look like an amateur compared to the men on *Duck Dynasty*, but his appearance would thwart the recognition software long enough to slip through. It didn't matter if the computer matched his face once he was over the border since he only needed a few hours' head start.

With his plan in mind, he sat up in bed and watched the news, but he quickly started dozing off, so he turned off the lights and tv.

A scream woke him.

Scott lay still.

The noise had sure sounded like a woman's scream, so he listened. A male voice, muffled, came through the wall. A man yelled, and a woman yelled back. Then she screamed again.

Stiletto didn't need anybody to draw him a picture. He was still dressed, so he rolled out of bed. With clenched fists, he left the motel room, took three steps to the neighboring room, and pounded on the door.

The door flew open, and a bony man with a dark goatee glared at him. A woman sobbed out of sight. The bony man raised a pointed finger, and Stiletto saw the blood on the man's knuckles. He grabbed the wrist and twisted, then pulled. The bony man let out a cry of his own as Stiletto hauled him out into the concrete walkway and kicked the man's legs out from under him. No snide remarks escaped Stiletto's lips. He delivered a hard punch to the bony man's face once, twice, and the skin under the man's left eye broke open. Stiletto lifted the man to his feet and twisted the arm back, forcing the man to face the wall, then shoved. The bony man left a smear of blood on the wall. Stiletto hammered two blows into the man's back. The man's breath rushed out, and he crumpled into a heap.

The woman was smaller, slight, and pale. She stepped into the doorway, and tears streaked her face. A bloody welt grew on her cheek. She put her hands to her mouth.

"Need a doctor?" Stiletto asked.

"Ohmygodohmygod," she said. She dropped her hands. "He's going to kill you!"

Other doors along the walkway opened, occupants poking out their heads to see the commotion. Somebody offered to call the cops, but Stiletto didn't answer. He suddenly wondered if he had done the right thing, but he didn't see how he couldn't have stepped in. This was the sort of incident he defined his philosophy by. Was he waiting for a thank you? He told the person offering to call the police to go ahead. They would ask Scott some questions, and his ID would hold up. He'd paid a lot of money for it to hold up under such scrutiny.

The woman rose and, letting out a rush of breath, went back into the room and slammed the door. She turned the lock. Her husband remained unconscious on the walkway, his face in a small pool of blood. Stiletto, feeling a little numb and not from the fight, returned to his room and locked the door. He sat on the edge of the bed and wondered if he had made the right decision after all.

He stood up and grabbed the tote bag, hurriedly stuffing his clothes and other items inside and pulling the zipper closed so fast he almost broke it. He did a quick scan to make sure nothing had been forgotten and, checking the walkway outside with a quick peek out the window, left the room. He stepped over the unconscious husband's body and hustled down the steps to the parking lot. He drove around the back of the building to the rear exit as a squad car pulling up in front of the building.

Stiletto found the interstate on-ramp and accelerated. His jaw was clenched, his breathing quick. He needed distance. He needed to get to Montreal. He didn't look back.

New York City

SUSAN STOOD in the bullpen watching her boss behind the glass wall of his office.

When she'd arrived three hours earlier, Brody

had told her and Ray to get their notes together because he wanted an update. While they gathered their reports, two muckity-mucks with government badges showed up and demanded a meeting of their own with only Brody. After an hour behind the glass, they were still in there flapping their gums and Susan was tired of impatiently tapping her feet.

"Sit down, Susan," Ray suggested.

She turned. Ray sat at his desk playing solitaire on his smartphone. The bullpen smelled of after-shave and coffee.

"Who are those guys?"

"Receptionist said they showed State Department ID."

"Then why aren't *we* in there? If this is about the Zubarev case, we should be in there."

"Sit down, Susan."

Susan let out a sigh and dropped into her chair. She fiddled with the pages in front of her, the Zubarev report as it stood so far, and absently read them once again. At least she could try to anticipate Brody's questions. Ray's face never left his smartphone as their colleagues hustled all around them. Somebody called for the blinds to be closed as the mid-afternoon sun blazed in and reflected blindingly off the glass behind which Brody and the other G-men sat. An agent seated near the window closed the blinds, and the room darkened a little.

Her desk phone buzzed. She picked it up. "This is Susan."

"Marjorie at the front desk," the receptionist said. "Somebody just brought you a package. They have it downstairs."

Downstairs, meaning the tech people were checking it for a bomb. Susan rubbed her temples. She'd forgotten all about the late-night phone call promising such a package. She said she'd be right down.

She updated Ray, left him to his solitaire, and took the elevator to the basement.

The overstuffed envelope had been scanned for explosives, cleared, and placed on a table in a small examining room with one of the fluorescent lights above flickering and making a clicking noise with each flash. Susan opened the package with her thumbnail and took out the stack of papers. Many were paperclipped or stapled together. Most of the writing was in English, but pages in Russian had attached translations. Some were pictures. As she read the first couple of pages, her heart started racing. This was the motherlode.

Her cell phone rang, and she dug it out of her pocket.

"Yes?"

"You should have the package by now."

"Mr. Olinov, I really need to see you."

"That is impossible. I'm at the airport."

"Where are you going?"

"I cannot tell you. It's for my own safety. You have what you need to finish your investigation. Do it in memory of me."

"Mr. Olinov— Hello?" She ended the call and found the man's number in the Received call list. She clicked on it and waited, but his voice mail answered. She left a message. "Please call me back. I have questions." She ended the call and figured that was the last she'd hear from him. *Do it in memory of me.* Wherever Yuri Olinov was going, he expected it to be a one-way trip.

Her hand was shaking when she put away her phone.

"Was it a note from a secret admirer?" Ray asked.

"Better," Susan replied. She told him all about it, and he came over to her side of the desk to get a better look. Susan's excitement overflowed. Her eyes were brighter and her earlier impatience at not being able to see Brody was gone, zeal taking its place. The muckity-mucks were still in Brody's office anyway, but at least now they had something solid to go over that wasn't yesterday's news.

"Look at this," Susan said. "A rundown on Russian organized crime in New York. I bet our own people don't have some of this stuff."

"We need a translator for these pages."

"Flip them over. It's been done."

Ray did, read, and whistled.

"But does anything specifically mention Zubarev?" he asked.

"Not that I've seen so far, but there is this little gem." Susan showed him a piece of paper with a woman's picture pinned to a corner. The photo showed an unsmiling brunette with short hair and a thin neck. "Siyana Antonova. Top assassin in the outfit. We need to talk to her."

"You want to try to interview an assassin?" Ray asked.

"Not interview her," Susan said. "Bring her in."

"We're gonna need some help."

Susan tapped the page. "We already have her address. We can call for backup along the way."

"But Brody—"

"Is still in his meeting." Susan gathered up the pages, jammed them back into the envelope, and stuck the envelope in a desk drawer, which she deftly locked. She rose from her chair and clipped her automatic to her belt. "Are you coming?"

She started for the exit with Ray at her heels.

"What's your theory?" Ray asked as Susan drove.

"Olinov sent us that information for a reason," she explained. "It ties in with Zubarev somehow. My thinking is Shishkin Pavlovitch, the local boss, sent Siyana Anton-whatever-her-name-is to kill not just Zubarev, but that other couple too."

"Where's Olinov now?"

"On a trip he doesn't expect to come back from."

Ray went silent for a moment, then, "This could be a trap."

"That's why we called for backup."

Ray had requested an FBI SWAT team as soon

as they hit the road. Normal protocol called for agents to file a formal request for such help and plan the arrest of high-threat suspects over a period of days, with surveillance covering the suspect until the last second. Ray had made his request from the field, calling it urgent, which meant they had no time for the normal formalities. The SWAT team would be there, but not necessarily when they arrived.

"I don't like this, Susan."

"We need to know what this woman knows. She's the key, I know it."

Presently Susan slowed the car for the turn from Allen Street onto Grand and parked curbside, the vehicle not straight, with the rear end sticking out a little. Susan and Ray exited the car. Across the street was a four-story apartment building. Susan consulted her notes. The hideout where Siyana Antonova lived was in the basement. The agents waited for a break in traffic and dashed across, walking around the side of the building to look for any basement access. There was none.

They worked around the back of the building, which was on a narrow alley with the next building right behind, and stopped at a gated door. Enough dust and debris covered the concrete in the alley, with a clear path from the door to the middle of the alley, to show that the door was accessed regularly. Susan turned the knob—locked. An electronic keycard sensor sat to the right.

Ray said, "We need to spoof that card reader or—"

"Nuts."

Susan pulled a folding leather pouch from her jacket and extracted a pair of lock picks, then knelt before the door and started working the knob while Ray stood lookout.

The locks popped, and Susan held the door open with her foot while she stowed her picks. No alarm sounded. Stairs went down. Susan moved forward and waited by the steps, taking out her automatic. Ray communicated with the SWAT commander.

"Team's still on the way," he said as Susan started down. Guns out, they stopped on the landing, looking at the hallway at the bottom of the steps.

Susan dropped into a squat and examined as much of the hallway as she could. It was short, with another door on the left side. Script on the door read Authorized Personnel Only.

"Come on," Susan said.

She started down the steps.

IT WAS A SPARTAN EXISTENCE, but Siyana had everything she needed and nothing she didn't.

She had long ago tempered the chill of the concrete floor with throw rugs, which added needed color to the space. The living room was a hair smaller than the bedroom, and a window might have been nice, but for somebody like her, who needed to keep a low profile and often used windows to the disadvantage of her targets, not having them was something she could easily live with. Plus, it meant one less thing to keep clean.

Siyana was lying in bed, staring at a spot on the ceiling. She had no plans for the day except to rest after so much activity, and then the red light started flashing. The red light was part of a panel on her nightstand, triggered by an electronic trip-wire in the stairwell. It meant somebody had broken through the door.

She threw off the covers and turned on the monitor atop the panel as she pulled jeans on over her pajama pants, tossing her top in exchange for a t-shirt. As she threw on a leather jacket with a pistol in a concealed pocket and other goodies in other pockets, the viewscreen showed the man and woman infiltrating her space.

She cursed. The whole building was owned by her boss, and every other floor was empty. It was her own personal sanctuary, but now she'd been discovered.

Siyana made a stop at the closet nearest the door for a submachine gun and let herself out.

As she advanced down the hallway, the lights on either side provided plenty of illumination, and she stopped at another panel to take care of that issue. She slowed her breathing and listened to the hesitant footsteps coming down the length of the hallway as they grew louder. She opened the panel and put a hand on the lever revealed behind the cover, then pulled it, and the lights went out.

Total darkness. The woman down the hall let out a yell and said somebody's name. Siyana, the enemy's position emblazoned in her mind, let the submachine gun rip. The muzzle flash filled the black void. Siyana's ears rang with the piercing echo of the salvo, but she didn't keep up the rate of fire for more than a second. Then, following a routine she had practiced many times, she turned and ran, headlong into the void for her alternate exit. The other end of the hall was outlined by a thin strip of Christmas lights so she could see the goal. The small green glow appeared quickly. A glance back showed bouncing flashlight beams—two of them. Had she missed? Siyana stopped, turned, and fired another burst, then made a fast sprint for the door, her lungs straining.

THE LIGHTS WENT OUT.

"Down, Ray!" Susan shouted. She dropped flat and heard Ray's body hit the ground as the fusillade of rounds came their way, bouncing off the walls and whistling down the length of the hall behind them. Susan grabbed her pocket flash and shined the light ahead, getting up to run with her pistol at the ready. Ray said something behind her, but she didn't hear. Another burst and another miss, and then Susan saw the green glow ahead.

Sunlight flooded the hall as the door opened, and Susan and Ray hit the deck again as Siyana fired. This time she was a target framed in the doorway, and Susan triggered a shot. The round sparked off the doorframe as Siyana turned and ran. Susan and Ray sprinted for the door, Susan easing it open and poking the barrel of her gun through. Siyana was running along the side of the building, and Susan and Ray gave chase, shouting for her to stop. She was a handful of yards from the street when she turned and swept the muzzle left to right, and Ray cried out and fell as slugs cut through him. Susan firing back, Siyana's head splitting as the 9mm projectile crashed through it. Her body fell back and the submachine gun slipped from her fingers as she hit the ground.

Susan ran to Ray. Blood seeped from a leg wound.

"I'm okay," he said through gritted teeth.

Susan ran to Siyana. The pool of blood beneath her head looked like a lake, and her eyes were open. There was nothing to be learned from the woman now.

Sirens and screeching tires on the other side of the building signaled the arrival of the cavalry.

Susan scoffed. Just in time, not that it would have made any difference.

CHAPTER 7

JIM BRODY, Susan's boss, had smoke coming out of his ears.

Maybe not literally, but if there was a time when that was going to occur, this was it.

"You had no business pursuing that lead," Brody snarled.

"What were we supposed to do, Jim?"

"You were supposed to stay in your seat and wait for me."

"Your meeting was taking forever."

"I don't understand your attitude, Susan."

"Maybe I'm pissed that Ray was shot."

"He only got shot because you two went into a situation you had no control over against a dangerous suspect with an automatic weapon. It falls under the category of 'shit happens.' You're lucky it wasn't worse."

Ray was still at the hospital getting his wound treated. He'd probably be off his feet for a week or two.

"I expect you to turn that report over to OrgCrime by the end of the day."

"It relates to my case, Jim."

"Not your case anymore."

"What?"

"That was what the meeting was about. Those men were top dogs at Justice and State, and they want us to lay off the Russians. Diplomatic problems and all that. They have a special investigator lined up to handle the Zubarev case, and we're not needed any longer."

"You accepted that garbage?"

Brody didn't shrug or make any kind of snide remark. His eyes remained soft as he looked at Susan.

"They pulled rank, Susan."

"They threatened you."

"Maybe."

"And this office?"

"Only me."

"Why?"

"They have their reasons. I know we have an investment in this, especially you and Ray, but it's not worth getting demoted or shucked off to nowhere because the government wants to go about this their own way."

Susan's mouth hung open.

"I tried," Brody continued, "but the decision was final."

"This is a cover-up."

"Might be, but it's out of our hands now. This office has other responsibilities, and we're expected to carry them out."

Susan closed her mouth and felt a red flush crawling up her neck.

"Take a few days and recharge," Brody ordered. "Go see Ray. When you return, we'll be back to normal, and you can forget this whole thing."

Susan rose from the chair and left Brody's office. She had no plans to forget about it. It wasn't in her nature. There were other ways of balancing the scales.

RAY, lying in his hospital bed with his leg in a cast, stared dumbly once Susan finished her update.

"That sucks," he said.

"You have an amazing way with words, Ray."

Susan stood beside his bed. The hospital room was the usual white and antiseptic décor, a wide doorway for the bathroom, and a tv mounted on the wall in front of the bed. Susan noticed a stack of books on the nightstand. Ray preferred reading to television.

Every few minutes they heard a page from the hallway speakers, each preceded by a ding.

"Well," he said, "it's not the first time we've had a case taken away."

"There's something about this one though, Ray. It's different."

"We have our orders."

"I know that."

"You're gonna hand over that file, right?"

"Sure," Susan said. "After I make a copy."

SUSAN LEFT the hospital and returned to the hotel, figuring on moving back to her apartment the next day and getting that cleaned up during her forced time off. She ordered dinner from room service and changed into a pair of sweats.

After she ate, she sat down and read her copy

of the Olinov file from beginning to end, soaking up the information. There were things she wanted to check out on her own time, but she'd have to be careful.

Before turning in, she used the hotel phone to make one call.

To her Uncle Ike.

CIA Headquarters

CARLTON WEBB WAS the Director of Central Intelligence, and his office was on the seventh floor of the headquarters building.

General Ike sat before the large desk.

"You have no idea where Stiletto has gone?" Webb asked.

Light blazed through the window that took up the wall to their left. The rest of the office was a mixture of wood for the floor and walls and leather for the furniture, with the United States flag behind Webb.

But General Ike did not sit in a leather chair or on the leather couch. He sat in a hard wooden chair in front of Webb's desk.

"He's off the installation, sir."

"And he's heading to Russia."

"I don't have any doubts about that."

"How can he get there?"

"David and I have been bouncing around possibilities," Fleming said. "Groups or individuals on the fringes may be of help if he can afford them."

"They'll also be the ones to try to cash in on the bounty."

"Exactly. His funds will be limited. He can't offer as much as we can."

"Any bites?"

"Nothing yet, sir."

"Should we alert the Russians?"

"Not at this time."

"Why are you so certain?"

"He can't enter the country through legal means," Fleming replied. "If our bounty doesn't uncover him, we can have our people in the region watch for him. He's good, but he's never faced the weight of this kind of search."

"That's too many ifs for me," Webb said. "I want our embassy in Moscow alerted at least."

"Don't do it through the usual channels. If the Russians are listening, they'll know the score."

"Send whoever you want."

"I'd like to send David McNeil, sir. He and Stiletto are friends. If David can't talk him out of this, nobody can."

"Hopefully he can do it without a fight."

"Stiletto won't fire on our people, sir."

"He beat the hell out of one of them.

"Note that the man is still alive."

Webb took a breath. "Ike, we need to zip this up before it goes to hell. That may mean using force on our end."

"I understand, sir."

"But will Scott?"

"He was smart enough to get as far as he has," Fleming replied. "He'll know what to expect if and when that time comes."

Canadian Border

STILETTO HAD no problems at the six-lane border crossing in Vermont. His beard had grown enough, and his hair didn't raise any eyebrows. If any cameras had captured him, he hadn't seen where they were located. He drove into Montreal at a moderate speed.

After the confrontation in New York, Stiletto

had stayed on the interstate for a few hours before pulling over at a rest area to sleep. Awakening with a sore neck, he continued driving, finding another motel to clean up at and have a decent meal. His mind was still buzzing with the consequences of his actions against the abusive husband. He had done the right thing; he was sure of it. But the fact that he had to keep telling himself that made him wonder if he *had* been right.

He crossed the St. Lawrence River via the Champlain Bridge around 9:30 p.m., the landscape and lit buildings of Montreal spreading out before him on all sides, and forced his mind to empty of all that had happened. He had to make contact with Hammond and find a way to get to Russia. That was all that mattered now.

He turned onto Rue St. Patrick and followed the roadway as it swept around a long curve, the Canal de Lachine off to his right and a warehouse district and construction zone on his left. Hammond owned a bar off Rue St. Patrick, with a clientele that ran heavily to the construction crowd, and he watched for the neon sign announcing the establishment. The bar was a stone's throw from the airport, where Hammond maintained a fleet of cargo planes under a cover name. Stiletto wanted to be on one of those planes, whichever was going toward Russia. He hoped he had enough cash to cover the ticket.

He reached the bar with the name Hammond's in bright neon out front and made a circle of the crowded parking lot, where there was not a space to be had. He pulled back onto the street and over on the right side of the road, then exited with his tote bag and jammed the Colt .45 in his belt before crossing the street.

The cool air touched the back of his neck, and he shivered. The water in the canal rippled quietly. This was hardly the place for a fight, but if Hammond required an impression, Stiletto had an idea of how to deliver one. Scott crossed the street at a trot, but instead of entering via the front door, he circled the building to the back. He smelled pungent cigarette smoke.

Two men stood near the back door in a makeshift smoking area, with a bucket for butts and some stray beer bottles lined up against the back wall. Stiletto rounded the corner and took a step toward the door. He expected the two men to let him pass, but they remained in place.

"Gotta go through the front, man," said one.

"Can't get in without paying the cover," said the other.

Stiletto kicked the closest one in the crotch.

The man doubled over, his cigarette hitting the ground along with a small amount of vomit as he upchucked tequila. The other tried to swing, but Stiletto's sharp sucker punch to the solar plexus took the breath and fight out of him. Scott added a sharp jab to the temple and the man dropped, unconscious.

Scott stepped over the bodies, the first still groaning in pain, and entered the back of the bar.

The narrow hallway had very little light, but the brightness ahead was the main bar, where voices and music battled for supremacy. More smoke and whiskey smells, then he passed a small kitchen where a short woman in a black apron juggled a trio of microwaves and a bunch of paper plates loaded with pre-cooked food. Across from that was an office marked Private. Stiletto opened the door to a small space with a cluttered desk and shelves. It smelled musty, and the tears in the chair behind the desk had been repaired with duct tape. Stiletto left the door open, turned on the lights, and sat behind the desk. He took out the .45 and set it amongst the clutter.

It didn't take long. As the woman in the apron passed the doorway carrying two of the paper plates, she stopped short and stuck her head in.

"What are you doing here? Get out."

"Get your boss."

"I'll get the bouncer."

Scott lifted the .45 and showed her the muzzle. "Get your boss."

The young woman blanched and hurried away.

Stiletto held the .45 in his lap and waited.

A hairy hand presently pushed the office door fully open. The rest of Jason Hammond was as hairy as the hand. The hair on his head was an overgrown helmet tied in the back, and his thick arms were furry up one side and down the other.

Hammond stood there with a bald man, the bouncer, behind him. The bouncer's plain blue t-shirt stretched tight across his body-builder frame.

"You're gonna wish you hadn't showed your face here, bub," Hammond said. The bouncer pushed past the smuggler but stopped when he found the .45 pointed at his gut.

"Chrome Dome can leave," Scott said. "I need to speak to you alone, Mr. Hammond."

Hammond let out a few curse words, but Scott didn't budge.

"It will be a profitable conversation, I promise," Stiletto continued.

"American dollars?"

"Of course."

"Beat it, Chrome Dome."

The bouncer grumbled at his boss but exited, and Hammond shut the door.

"You're in my seat."

"You've been sitting all night."

"Okay, okay. I'll stand here and look like an idiot. At least put the piece down."

Stiletto complied.

"You could have some in the front door, you know," the Canadian said.

"The bartender would still be telling me he's never heard of you."

"Touché."

"I need to get into Russia, and you have planes that go that way. How much?"

"I don't even know who you are."

"The name on my passport is Peter Drumm."

"That can't be your real name."

"At least I didn't tell you it was Smith."

"Or Jones. I get a lot of guys named Jones. They tell me they're all related."

"How much?"

"How much do you have?"

Stiletto pulled the tote bag onto his lap and unzipped it. He flashed some of his cash. "Twenty grand."

"I'll take nineteen," Hammond agreed. "Leave you some eating money." He laughed. "My next flight in that direction doesn't leave for another forty-eight hours."

Stiletto bit off a curse. He was taking way too long to get to Moscow. Glinkov could be dead by now.

"Okay," Scott said.

There was a knock at the door, then a female voice asked, "Everything okay, Jason?"

Hammond opened the door and let the woman in. She had dark hair and brown eyes, and wore a blouse and skirt combo that seemed way out of place for where they were. Her black hair framed her pretty face very nicely, and she had a small nose and mouth. Her lips shone with red lipstick.

"This is Kim Cortner, my assistant manager, who dresses way too nice for this dump,"

Hammond said. "Kim, meet Peter Drumm. We're going to give him a ride to Russia."

"Are you paying cash?" she asked.

Hammond laughed. "One track mind, this girl."

Stiletto smiled. "Know a place I can stay tonight? Nearby?"

"I got a spare room upstairs," Hammond said. "Ain't five-star, but it's a cot, and there's a toilet here."

"I'll take it."

"Kim will show you where it is."

"Follow me," the woman directed.

Scott put his gun away, and Hammond moved out into the hall to let Stiletto and the woman pass. He followed her back down the hall to an alcove that had a door at the end, the door revealing access to the second floor. There was even less light in the narrow stairwell but they managed, the woman pushing open the only door on the top landing. Scott turned on the light. White walls, bare floor, cot with a wool blanket in the corner against the wall.

"This will work fine," he said.

"You'll have the place to yourself once we leave," the woman told him. "But I wouldn't wander downstairs. We have motion-detectors that will set off an alarm. Small bathroom is down the hall. You won't need much else."

Stiletto let out a breath. He wasn't in any mood to argue about leaving for somewhere nicer. Nobody could find him here.

WHEN HE AWOKE the next morning, the only thing that gave any indication of a new day was the date on his watch. The room had no windows, although cool air blew through a floor vent. He heard voices through the vent, mostly muffled. He didn't try to make out the words but instead rose, found the small bathroom down the hall, and cleaned up with a washcloth and hot water. The cot had been okay. He'd find a real hotel to hole up while waiting for Hammond's plane. Another night was out of the question.

When he returned to the room, Kim was sitting on the cot with her legs crossed. "Hello," she said.

Stiletto grinned, and she brought up a gun from behind her back.

"Get in the corner."

Somebody shoved Scott from behind. He started to fall, but arrested the descent and dropped to his hands and knees instead. He turned his head. Jason Hammond stood in the doorway with two men, both of whom were quite fit in their dark suits.

"I'll use English," Hammond said. "Your measly nineteen grand couldn't compete with the one million offered by your agency, *Mister* Stiletto."

Stiletto rose to his feet.

Hammond said, "These two men are from your embassy, and they'll be happy to take you back over the border."

"Don't make any trouble, Stiletto," one of the suited men warned.

Scott said, "May I at least put on my shoes? Gonna be a long drive."

The agency men said okay and watched, and Kim's Beretta .25 automatic didn't waver as Stiletto tied his shoes. One of the embassy men grabbed the tote bag, checked the contents, and zipped it. Stiletto went quietly. The embassy officers took him outside to a waiting Lincoln sedan, shiny and black in the sun, the windows tinted. For all he knew, General Ike sat in the back seat.

The canal lay across the road.

The two embassy men walked beside him,

neither going for a weapon nor speaking. They crossed the parking lot to the Lincoln, and Stiletto made up his mind. These two suited ciphers weren't going to stop him from getting to Russia any more than the surveillance team outside the bank.

Stiletto snapped up his left elbow, twisting his body and putting some force into the blow. The elbow struck the embassy man in the right shoulder, spinning him like a top as he let out a yell. Scott launching a low kick into the other man's upper leg and both went down, although the first scrambled to his feet, yelling at Scott as he snatched up the tote bag and ran for his car. He heard more sounds behind him and then gunfire, several rapid shots from a pistol.

Scott looked back as he charged forward. Hammond and Chrome Dome were aiming automatics at him, the shots kicking up the dirt. He started zigzagging. He was no good to them dead, and as he neared the car and felt in the tote bag for the car keys, he realized he had nowhere to go without those. Somebody must have removed them. Stiletto shifted away from the car, the next salvo punching into the bodywork. He aimed for the canal.

His shoes hammered the pavement, then he leaped down the short slope from the road into the water, splashing across to the other side. No more shots came his way. Stiletto climbed up the other side and continued across the pavement, shoving through a tear in a chain-link fence to run across the blacktop of a warehouse with big rigs backed up against a loading dock and a line of cars in a parking lot. Stiletto spotted a man getting into his car. Scott might not have had keys, but he had his .45, and he grabbed it out of the tote and ran up to the man.

"Get away!"

The man yelled and shuffled back, falling over and landing hard. Stiletto opened the driver's door, pulled the keys from the lock, and tossed his tote bag on the passenger seat. He had the Ford in motion seconds later, tires screaming. They left a black patch of rubber and a trail of smoke as he steered toward the exit.

Stiletto was sweating; he felt the trickles down his back and neck and under his arms. He was also breathing fast, his pulse rate seemingly as out of control as the situation in which he found himself. What did he do now?

Stiletto followed the road to a four-way intersection, where he was forced to stop, a big rig crossing in front of him. The big rig cleared the intersection, and Stiletto started across. That was when the other car collided with the back quarter-panel of the Ford, slamming the unbelted Stiletto across to the passenger side door and sending the vehicle spinning off the road.

Senses began returning ever so slowly, like the tingling sensation when a numb limb comes back to life. He was flat on his back on something soft, but he could move his arms and legs. No restraints. His eyes opened, his vision foggy at first. The light in the room caused throbbing near his temples.

He wiped his eyes. He was in a hotel room, the window and drapes shut and the room very quiet. Something moved near the door, and Stiletto saw a black man looking at him. The man wore a dark suit. He pressed a button on a cell phone and spoke into it.

"He's awake, sir." He paused. "Yes, sir."

The guard put the phone away.

"Everything will be fine, Mr. Stiletto," the

guard said. "Just relax, and my bosses will be here in a few moments."

Stiletto took the time to explore his body. He was sore all over from the impact of the car, but nothing appeared to be broken. He wondered if he had a slight concussion.

"Who hit me?" Stiletto said.

"I don't know," the guard replied.

The door opened, and three old men entered. They wore suits as well, heads either bald or white-haired, eyes sharp but showing their age.

"You're in one piece, Mr. Stiletto," said the leader of the trio. He spoke slowly, his voice low. He was far beyond the age where one needed to hurry his words.

"Where am I?"

"At a much nicer location than that dreadful bar."

The man dismissed the guard, who left quietly and shut the door behind him. The man stood near the foot of Scott's bed, while the other two found seats at the table. They sat with the relief of those who can't be on their feet for long periods, but that did not seem to affect the spokesman.

"You're at a Hilton," the older man said. "One of the regular rooms, I'm afraid. We didn't want to arouse any more attention than we already had by carrying you in like a drunk."

"Whoever was in the other car hit me too hard."

"We've dealt with them. I told the driver you were no good to us hurt. Would you like some tea and a moment to clean up?"

"I'd rather know who you are." Stiletto sat up against the headboard. He still felt dizzy, so he kept his head still.

The old man smiled. "Of course. You may refer to me as Number One. My colleagues are Numbers Two and Three. Our identities must remain a secret, and you'll know why soon enough."

Stiletto nodded.

"And I daresay," Number One continued, "if you knew our names, you'd know far too much about what we're doing."

"Uh-huh."

"But you aren't impressed. Somebody of your rank knows too much of what goes on. You wouldn't notice our tiny efforts at all.

"We are known as The Trust," the man continued. "More than the three of us, certainly, but we were the nucleus. We're a group of retired intelligence professionals who unfortunately know the failings of the organized intelligence community and formed to act in such a way as the bureaucracies cannot. We have a cadre of operatives all over the world, in every country. You cannot go anywhere and not have a friend, if you know what I mean."

"Never heard of you," Scott told him.

"Exactly." Number One smiled. "But we have certainly heard of you, Mr. Stiletto. We know what you're doing. We've brought you here since our interests in Russia are mutual."

"Do tell?"

"What's happening there is of great concern to us, since we sponsored a lot of the coup plotters' activities. I don't know if you've been watching the news, or even had time, but most of the plotters have been rounded up. There are only a few who remain free. We'd like to help you get into the country."

"What's the catch?" Stiletto said.

"No catch. Find your friend and help his family get out. We'd like to get what's left of our people out too. In return, we'll help you get in, provide cover, and help you get out. Any problems you have with the CIA are up to you to handle. You made that bed."

"I'm well aware of that, thanks. What I really want to know is how you found me."

"We have people everywhere, inside and outside the intelligence community, who keep their eyes open for us."

"That doesn't answer my question."

"Okay, perfectly blunt: you should send Mr. Fleming a thank-you note."

"General Ike?"

"He issued the bounty," Number One explained. "All we had to do was wait until somebody called to claim it. You're lucky we got here as fast as we did or, should I say, the embassy moved as slow as it did."

"He's part of your group?"

"Has been for quite a few years, and I'll get no thanks from him for telling you that." Number One took a breath. "There are times when problems must be solved without red tape, and Mr. Fleming is smart enough to know that."

"Bastard talks out of both sides of his mouth."

"You can't really blame him," Number One admonished.

"I'll try not to."

"You'll work with us?"

Stiletto nodded. "Yes."

"If the worst happens, and you're forced out of the Agency, you will be welcome in our organization. We pay a stipend, of course. You won't be kept from pursuing your own interests, either, should something come up. Or you can walk away entirely. I understand you have options in San Francisco?"

"I don't know if they're *options*, but something like that, yeah."

"Do you need time to think it over?"

"No," Scott said. "If my career goes belly-up and you're the only ticket in town, we'll talk. But let's get Russia over with first. We're running out of time. My friend is running out of time."

"I am very pleased to hear that. We have a few arrangements to make, and you need to rest a little. Enjoy the room. Your bag is over there, and we'll provide any other equipment you might need or replace whatever is missing. Also, I'll have some tea sent up. You look like you need it."

The other two men, who had oddly remained silent during the entire chat, stood from their chairs, and Number One bid Scott a good rest.

Then the three old men filed out and shut the door quietly behind them.

Stiletto started to laugh, but that hurt, so he stopped. Of all the twists he could have tried to predict, this wasn't one of them.

And he'd indeed have to find some way of communicating with General Ike. The old warhorse had been on his side the whole time.

Stiletto tentatively stood, putting a hand on the wall. When he didn't fall over, he made his way to the bathroom.

CHAPTER 8

Moscow

David McNeil looked out the window at the passing street. Moscow had certainly changed in the last fifteen years.

He'd passed through on assignment now and then after the turn of the century, watching the city and country rebuild from Communism, and the number of cars in the street suggested things were chugging along decently on the economics side. The lack of statues of Soviet pioneers was a nice touch, as was the explosion of color and the erasure of Moscow's Soviet drabness. It had frankly been depressing.

He stood in an office on the upper floor of the

US Embassy in Moscow, the property inside the walls busy with staffers and Marine guards.

It was the office of the local agency attaché in charge of the in-country case officers who were, in turn, in charge of their various informants and spies within the Russian government. Some things never changed.

The man behind the desk, Joe Wilcox, was younger, with a full head of black hair and eager brown eyes. His tie remained snug in his collar. Wilcox's glasses reflected the glare of his computer screen as he scrolled through files.

"I don't see any mention of Stiletto or any other stray American in any of our reports," Wilcox said. "Are you sure he's heading here?"

"It's our educated guess," McNeil said, not turning from the window. "Nothing has come in from St. Petersburg or anywhere else?"

"Not during the timeframe you've given me," Wilcox replied.

McNeil turned from the window. His artificial leg had set off the metal detectors when he'd entered the building that day, resulting in an awkward situation for the Marines as they made him show the leg. He didn't mind; he knew they had to check. At least nobody had tried tapping it with a nightstick.

His cell phone had been confiscated per embassy policy (one in effect globally), so the only way he could reach General Ike or vice versa was through the landlines, which he didn't trust. Wilcox assured him they swept for bugs regularly and that they hadn't had any incidents in the three years he'd been assigned to the post.

"What if something happened to Stiletto on the way?"

"I'd be very upset," McNeil told him.

The phone rang. Wilcox answered and told McNeil the call was for him.

General Ike asked, "What's your status, David?"

"No sign of Stiletto or any stray American in any of our regular reports," McNeil told his boss. "Anything on your end?"

"Montreal," Fleming said, and explained how Scott had been in custody for mere minutes before stealing a car. "Now we have no idea where he is."

"If he knows about the bounty, he knows he's blown. He'll have no choice but to come back. Did Hammond keep the money?"

"Our embassy people exercised some force and reacquired the cash."

"But what about Scott?"

"He's made no attempt to contact us. If he wants to come in, he knows how to reach me. For now, we have to assume he'll remain on the run long enough to find an alternate means of transportation. If that fails, I expect him to call."

"How long do you want me to stay here?"

"Until further notice," Fleming said, "because I have a side job for you."

Fleming took a few minutes to explain the "Olinov File" delivered to him by his FBI-agent niece, and the details therein about the connections between Russian political leaders and the Mafia—especially overseas. "Look into it. You might find Scott that way."

"All right, sir. Moscow's nice this time of year."

McNeil hung up the phone. Wilcox's eyes were glued to the computer.

"Something on your mind?" McNeil asked.

"Looking at a map. You mentioned St. Petersburg, and that got me thinking."

"It's the best point of entry. The other routes would take him through Europe and Asia, and he's not going to do that."

"I'm going to order a little more attention to be focused on St. Petersburg," Wilcox said. "You might be right."

"As long as the Russians don't tip to what we're doing. Are your informants trustworthy?"

Wilcox frowned. "Are you kidding? We have informants checking on our informants. We're in Russia, for heaven's sake!"

McNeil nodded. "Some things never change."

CABIN FEVER WAS SETTING IN.

And there was nothing Dimitri Ravkin could do about it.

Anastasia continuously paced the room, barely sitting down long enough to catch her breath. Rina was getting depressed and barely holding together, her daughter clutched her teddy bear for dear life, and all Ravkin could do was wait for an email that would let them know help was coming. Anastasia's suggestion of getting fake identities and passports for them had been shot down. There was no way they'd last on the street long enough to get that done, and even if they did, transportation centers would be watched, and Ravkin knew of nobody who was free to get them out of the country.

Ravkin sat in a corner of the room with his laptop, furiously typing instant messages with several contacts who had survived the round-up and were still managing to do their regular jobs. Either the FSB didn't know about them or they were under surveillance, although neither of them had reported seeing anybody following them.

Ravkin wanted to know where the government was holding Glinkov. Nobody knew. Ditto their other captured comrades.

Or maybe they *weren't* being held, and instead had been immediately shot.

Ravkin took a different line of questioning. Assuming they were still alive, they might be on the wrong trail by focusing only on where the government might take them. What about the Mafia? What secret interrogation areas had sprung up that the grapevine hadn't learned of yet? Somebody on the street should know.

Ravkin's contacts promised to get back to him.

He left the corner and found Anastasia with her arms folded, staring at him from across the room.

"What's on your mind?" He tried to keep the edge out of his voice.

"What did you learn?"

"Nothing."

"Nothing? After all that, you know nothing?"

"We know where Glinkov *isn't*," Ravkin told her. "We don't know where he *is*."

"And what about us? We're choking in this place."

"Another couple of days."

"That's not good enough."

Rina Glinkov wandered in from down the hall, her face drawn and stress in her eyes. "Why are you arguing again?"

Anastasia said, "Because Mr. Ravkin still knows nothing, and continues to insist we stay in this pillbox."

"Help is on the way," Ravkin assured them.

"What does that mean?" Anastasia asked.

"Our benefactors will be on touch soon."

"We don't have any benefactors, Dimitri."

"There is so much about this you don't know, Anastasia. That Glinkov doesn't know. We have to be patient."

The laptop let out a beep, and Ravkin smiled. "That might be the message we're waiting for."

Ravkin went to the laptop, conscious of Anastasia and Rina crowding over his shoulder.

He opened an email from Number One.

"Who is this?" Anastasia said. "Who is Number One?"

"A friend."

Ravkin read the email twice and let out a whistle.

"Who is this Stiletto?" Anastasia asked, "and why are you the one who gets to meet him?"

"I know who he is," Rina said. "One of Vlad's American friends."

Ravkin sniffed.

"So the Americans are coming," Anastasia grumbled. "Is that supposed to make me feel better?"

"He'll get us out of the country, Ana," Ravkin explained. "Isn't that what you want?"

"What if he gets us all killed?"

"Then you won't have any reason to pace the floor like a caged animal, will you?"

"Gavnoyed."

Ravkin snapped. "Go sit somewhere away from me before I shove you through the wall."

Anastasia opened her mouth again, but Rina cut her off.

"Stop this right now! If there is help, there is hope. That is what we have to hang onto right now, not fight each other."

Ravkin and Anastasia's eyes remained locked, but she broke contact first and moved away.

THE DC-9 WASN'T Stiletto's first choice for transportation, but beggars couldn't be choosers and all that.

The roar of the propellers filled the cabin, but luckily he had earplugs, provided by the pilot. Number One had delivered the promised gear, including a parachute, replacement cash, a satellite phone for emergency contacts, and ammo for his pistol. He'd also managed to provide Scott with a sketchbook and a couple of pens, but as he sat on the hard chair near a window, the occasional turbulence prevented his hand from drawing steadily. Eventually, he decided that his usual careful drawings could morph into fuzzy modern art for this trip, but the amusement didn't last long, and he set the sketchbook aside.

Stiletto did squats in the aisle every now and then. He was the only person in the passenger cabin, and that novelty had quickly worn off too. He'd never been a serious practitioner of the social arts, but after so many days on the run and alone, he sure wanted some conversation.

The pilots sat up front with the cockpit door firmly shut. They didn't want him intruding, and he understood that. It was a long flight into hostile territory, and they were in as much danger as he was.

He did some more squats, challenged not only by bending his knees deeper each time but keeping his balance as the DC-9 rocked. He dropped into a chair, breathless from the effort, and when his breathing returned to normal, he started checking his parachute for the umpteenth time.

He returned to sketching but gave up again to stare out the window. The earplugs reduced the engine noise to a dull throb, and after so many hours, his head hurt from the incessantly pounding. They were still over the ocean, although he wasn't sure where. He had no idea how long it would be until they reached Russian airspace and the drop zone over St. Petersburg where Number One had said somebody would meet him.

Scott hoped the message reached the agent on the Russian end or he'd be in huge trouble.

THE POLICE CAR flashed by at a high rate of speed. Sweat covered Ravkin's neck and back despite the blasting air conditioner and the cold temperatures outside. His headlamps blazed along the highway toward St. Petersburg, and his GPS said he was on time. Might even arrive a little early. Ravkin didn't know which he preferred, or if arriving late would be better to make sure the American was there. All he knew was that the police car had been traveling along the last few miles, not bothering him or any other car, and his mind had been filled with images of being pulled over and shot at any moment. But apparently something more important came along, and the police car sped down the road. Hopefully, there wasn't an accident that would slow Ravkin down. Possibly the cop would take one of the next exits and have to deal with a problem on city streets.

Ravkin wiped one sweaty hand on his jeans, then the other, and took a deep breath as he settled both on the wheel and finally started to calm down.

There had been many close shaves in his career as an FSB agent, from chasing criminals and winning convictions to having a gang put a contract on his head. All of them paled in comparison to what he was doing now: putting his life on the line for a shot at a better Russia. It would have been so much easier not to bother. Then the Trust had joined the effort and made them feel like they were part of a bigger apparatus. Which might have been true, but that support system couldn't keep Putin's machine from discovering the plot.

There was probably no way to salvage the operation, Ravkin realized. All their work had been for naught, but they could get out of Russia and start over somewhere else. He wasn't sure what his future might look like, but even the unknown was better than the certain death he faced if he remained in Moscow or anywhere else in the country.

Six hours later with a rest stop or two in between, Ravkin finally arrived at St. Petersburg Port. He drove along the frontage road to the east end of the port and through the open gate beside an empty office building, as instructed. He aimed the car at the water ahead, which rippled next to the jetties. Ships sat in the docks, cranes for the shipping containers stretching into the sky, but no bodies lurked at this late hour. When Ravkin parked and shut off the car, the silence made the hair on the back of his neck stand up. The water made its splish-splash noises, but that was all. Not even the wind carried any hint of life within a mile of his spot.

He'd parked in the space between two buildings, which let him see part of an empty dock and moonlight reflecting off the water. That was the spot the American was expected to emerge from. They would exchange a crude signal phrase and make the long drive back to Moscow. Ravkin's heart raced as he sat still.

THE FUSELAGE DOOR opened and cold air rushed in. Stiletto stepped toward the opening. He'd checked his rig a hundred times, so there was nothing more he could do except trust the gear and leap into the void.

And "void" was the correct word. As he stood framed in the doorway awaiting the co-pilot's signal to jump, the sea below and the sky above appeared pitch-black, as if he were jumping into nothing. Then the lights of the port appeared on his right.

Stiletto's tote bag and weapons were strapped to either leg, tied tight to prevent them from going bye-bye during freefall. He also wore a facemask to keep his eyes from being sucked out. The rubber seal on his left cheek felt a little wonky, though, so he expected it to fail and let air in. As long as the Plexiglas portion didn't fail, he'd be fine.

The co-pilot gave him the go signal as the plane flew over their designated drop zone. All doubts exited Stiletto's mind as he stepped through the opening and began his high-speed fall back to Earth.

THE COLD WIND blew through Stiletto's jumpsuit and pulled at the mask. The left cheek seal indeed broke a little, and the extra chill on his face invigorated him. He steered his body to the right. The miles-long port below was all lit up, and he was falling like a bomb at a hundred and twenty miles per hour.

He straightened his body and aimed toward the eastern side of the port, where there was a marsh and relatively shallow water. The person Number One said would meet him, a man named Ravkin, should have arrived by now.

Scott had decided on the parking lot as his primary landing spot, with the marsh as the backup. His trip would be over really quickly if there were FSB agents waiting to arrest him rather than a contact waiting to pick him up, but it was too late to reconsider. Much too late. Stiletto would have to play whatever hand he was dealt, but the old man had given the briefing confidently, and Scott knew he was no fool. They would not have bothered sending him if they'd known the effort was hopeless, or worse, compromised. A good agent could turn a hopeless situation around, but a compromised operation was doomed from the start.

Number One had not said much about Ravkin other than that he was a Trust member and part of the effort to overthrow Putin. Not all of the coup plotters were Trust people, but there were enough salted through the organization to keep the information flowing.

Stiletto continued his rapid descent, the landing zone growing larger by the second, and he pulled the ripcord. The parachute billowed out of the pack and deployed into a perfect canopy, pulling at Scott's harness, the violent jolt rocking his entire body. As he maneuvered the control risers, he looked down at the packs strapped to either leg. They were still there.

The ground rushed to meet him and he pulled the risers sharply, slowing his drop a fraction more as his feet hit hard on the pavement. He didn't fall. Ahead of him, headlights flashed on and off. A sinking feeling took over, but he bundled the 'chute in his arms anyway.

The car approached slowly, and Stiletto breathed easier. The FSB would have brought more than one vehicle.

The car stopped, and the driver's window went down. The man had both hands tight on the wheel, and his nervous eyes locked on Scott's as he removed his facemask.

"This is an odd spot for a vacation," the man said. His voice shook a little.

"It's my Number One choice," Stiletto answered.

"Ravkin." The Russian stuck out a hand.

"Later," Scott replied. "Pop the trunk."

With the chute stowed in the back, Stiletto joined Ravkin in the car and the Russian steered for the exit.

DAVID MCNEIL HADN'T MADE a covert pickup in years. He sat in the back seat of the dark embassy car holding a tray containing two cups of steaming coffee, street lights flashing into the cabin as they traveled.

The back seat of the sedan was quite plush, the

insulation making the drive quiet. When the driver finally pulled over, McNeil looked around, uncertain where they actually were. He had no guard and no sidearm, but he wasn't expecting the meeting to go south. Of course, he hadn't expected to lose his leg, either.

McNeil cleared his throat as the door opened. A small man in a black coat slid into the car and pulled the door shut. The driver started off again. McNeil passed the man one of the coffee cups.

"Thank you," the man said. He took a sip. "Odd that you wanted to meet so late."

"I figured it was best," McNeil said. "Did you have a chance to look into what I asked?"

The small man sipped his coffee again. He had short-cropped black hair and dark eyes, but the rest of his features were obscured by the darkness of the cabin. The flashing street lamps highlighted his small features, and McNeil couldn't look away from the man's crooked nose.

Anatoly Petrov worked in the Ministry of Justice. The Agency had recruited him years ago when his daughter was sick and he was having a hard time getting the medicine she needed in a country still transitioning from Communism. The local embassy case officer had stepped in, the girl received the needed medications, and the Americans had a new deep-cover asset.

He hadn't flinched when McNeil had asked him about any intelligence that could tie Vladimir Putin to the Russian Mafia and whether he used them as his personal assassins.

"No hard data," Petrov said. "A lot of rumors, but nothing we can substantiate. Putin puts nothing on paper. If he's doing it, it's all done by proxy."

"Of course it's done by proxy, but we need something tangible."

"It's not there."

"Who might have something?"

"The Mob."

"Really?"

"They're stupid like that," the Russian said quietly. "They think they're protected from on high, and we can't get anybody inside."

"Why?"

"They always get tipped off. We've lost three undercovers trying."

McNeil let out a breath and looked out the window. "You probably have the same answer to my other question."

"Yes. If Putin is using the Russian mob overseas, there's no indication on our end. He knows the diplomatic risk."

"Another proxy."

"Somebody will talk one of these days."

McNeil turned back to the Russian. "I can't wait that long."

"You're thinking of the Zubarev case."

"Exactly."

Petrov only nodded. "You can drop me anywhere. I'll get a cab back."

"THERE'S no way we can go after the local mob bosses," Joe Wilcox, McNeil's contact at the US Embassy, said.

"Our people might get farther than the FSB," McNeil told him. "You can't betray somebody you don't know about."

"You're right, but first you have to convince your boss, who will have to convince the director, and when he asks you why, you'll have some explaining to do."

"What do you mean by that?"

"Are you trying to help Stiletto or catch him?"

"Maybe a little bit of both."

They sat in Wilcox's office. The embassy chief

was obviously tired, and he had his sleeves rolled up and tie loosened. McNeil still wore the long overcoat and he once again stood at the window looking out into the night, as if the answers to his questions were somewhere in the shadows stretching along the street.

"I'm useless here," McNeil said.

"We both need a night's rest," Wilcox countered.

McNeil sighed as the embassy man turned off his desk lamp and followed him out of the office.

"Let's have another pass at this in the morning," Wilcox said. "What we have to do is convince the boss that the Zubarev situation means we have to investigate on this end."

"They already cut off the FBI. They won't budge unless we can bring them something."

"Well, I'm fresh out of smoking guns, David."

CHAPTER 9

"How much did Number One tell you?" Ravkin asked.

"Everything, I think," Scott replied.

"You know it's only me and one other, plus Glinkov's wife and kid?"

Stiletto's voice was grim. "Yes. Any luck finding where Vlad is being held?"

Glinkov might have been milked dry and killed by now. The goal should be to get Ravkin and his crew out of the country. If Glinkov was gone, there was nothing they could do for him anyway, but Scott wouldn't commit to that thought. If there was still a chance he was alive, they had to try to find him.

They were one of the few cars on the road, and none of the other cars took any notice of them.

"Nobody's following us?" Scott said.

"We've been very lucky."

"I hate that word."

"Right. You never know when it's going to run out."

Presently they arrived at the building where Anastasia and Glinkov's family were hiding in the basement. Ravkin led Scott through the building's concrete underground garage to where the fluorescent lights flickered and ominous corner shadows dared to taunt. Ravkin used a passcode on a door marked Authorized Personnel Only in Cyrillic and led Scott down a dimly-lit corridor.

The door opened into another short corridor that led to a furnished room, warmed only by a humming space heater. A television was playing in a corner, and a woman paced the floor. She stopped and faced Stiletto and Ravkin with her arms folded.

"Is this the American?"

"It is."

"Hello," Scott said.

Ravkin made the introductions, but Anastasia

made no move to shake hands. She examined Scott without blinking.

"Have you seen the news?" she asked.

Ravkin and Stiletto moved to the television, where the news was on, and Ravkin translated. There had been more arrests related to the planned coup, and a statement from the FSB was expected any minute.

Stiletto began, "Does this mean—"

"He might still be alive, yes."

"Or," Anastasia said, coming over to them, "he's dead, and they got information from somebody else."

"Have they released any names?" Ravkin asked. "That might give us a clue."

"Who cares?" Anastasia replied. "Now that our American hero is here, we need to get out of Russia. The longer we stay, the more danger we are in."

Another voice joined the conversation. Another woman.

"I'm not leaving Russia without my husband."

Stiletto rose. The new arrival was more haggard than Stiletto had ever seen a woman look, and she oozed stress. There was no doubt about her identity.

"Rina."

"You are Scott?"

"Yes."

She hugged Stiletto weakly. "Vlad talks about you all the time."

"I'm sorry I'm late."

"He knew you'd come."

"Your daughter?"

"She's down the hall, asleep."

Ravkin said, "Here they are."

The group turned to the tv. It wasn't Putin in front of the podium this time, but a representative from the FSB. They announced the arrest of three more of the plotters, and provided names and the details of how they had been captured.

"Who are they?" Stiletto asked as the FSB man droned on.

"Not key leaders like he's saying," Ravkin said. "They're lying."

Anastasia added, "Foot soldiers and logistics people."

"Would Vlad know of them?"

Ravkin shook his head.

"The FSB either caught them on their own, or somebody else other than Vlad cracked."

Rina asked, "He's still alive?"

Anastasia snapped off the television. "That doesn't matter. We need to get out of this country now. I had a plan," she said to Stiletto, "but this one"—sharp point at Ravkin—"said no."

"What was the plan?" Stiletto asked.

"Fake passports and a train," Ravkin explained.

"Is that any more than your phantom benefactors will do?"

"Probably not," Ravkin said, "but it won't be us going out on the street to get them." He turned to Scott. "What did Number One tell you to do?"

"Get you all out of here, with Vlad, if I can."

"They have an exfil plan?"

"I have to call them first."

Rina said, "We aren't going anywhere without my husband."

Nobody spoke for a moment, but their eyes were on each other, anger mixed with suspicion and uncertainty.

"Any chance," Stiletto asked, "that I could get a cup of tea?"

ANASTASIA AND RAVKIN went to get tea and coffee for everybody while Stiletto talked to Rina.

They sat close on the couch with the tv still on but the sound off.

"Do you understand me?" Rina asked. "You all seem to think I'm joking."

"Nobody's going anywhere until we have a look at where Vlad might be. That was why I came all this way. Never mind what's-her-ass."

Rina smiled a little.

Ravkin and Anastasia returned with steaming mugs, and Stiletto took his tea while the others had coffee. Ravkin and Anastasia pulled chairs closer to the couch.

"What do you know for sure?" Stiletto asked.

"Vlad is not being held officially anywhere in Moscow," Ravkin said. "He might be in some mob hideout somewhere, and I have contacts looking into that."

"Any of those contacts arrested tonight?"

Ravkin shook his head. "No."

"Why are the two of you still on the street?"

"Nobody knows about this place," Ravkin told him. "Not even Vlad. This is *my* safehouse."

"I've made it clear to Rina that I'm here to get Vlad out if he's still alive," Stiletto said. "Our mutual friend asked me to get you out as well, and whoever was with you. I don't know exactly how, or what to do with you once we reach the States. You're doing something illegal, so you can't claim asylum."

"The Trust will take care of everything."

"You have enormous faith in them."

"They've delivered for us, this present situation notwithstanding."

Anastasia asked, "Are you ever going to tell me who you're talking about?"

Stiletto looked at Ravkin, who nodded and told the story of the Trust and his connections to Number One. Anastasia listened without interrupting. When Ravkin finished, she seemed a little less pissed off.

"Did Vlad know?" Rina asked.

Ravkin shook his head. "Just me."

Rina nodded.

Ravkin looked at Scott. "The US will do whatever I tell them once they see the intelligence I'm bringing."

"Which is what?" Scott asked.

"Evidence of the conspiracy between Putin and the Mafia. We were planning to use it when the coup took place since it made the case for what we needed to do, but now that information can be used to save me, Anastasia, and Vlad's family."

"Hell," Scott said, "it might even save me. Where is this information?"

"In the cloud. No hard disk or documents. You need a password to access it, and your people can have that when we're safe on US soil."

"If you're bluffing, they'll send you back."

"It's not a bluff."

"We're waiting to hear from your contacts, correct?"

"Yes," Ravkin said.

Stiletto downed what remained of his tea. "Then we better get some rest, or try to. I'll probably sleep like a log after all I went through to get here."

SCOTT LAY on the cot in the small room at the very end of the hall.

Ravkin finally talking about the Trust seemed to put the women at ease. Anastasia in particular had calmed down, and some of the stress had gone out of Rina's eyes. He hoped beyond hope that there was something of Vlad to bring back. Perhaps he'd only have the kind of scars that would heal over time.

He rolled onto his side and shifted to get

comfortable. The cot was narrow, and the springs on either side of the frame dug into him. It sure beat sleeping in the mud, however.

And then there was Ravkin's revelation about the cloud. Scott wanted that to be true. It would indeed help his case when he returned to the US. He'd still be in debt to the Trust, but like his boss, there would be ways to help on the sly.

That was his last thought before he dozed off.

The lone bathroom across from his room was about the size of a closet, but Stiletto showered in the morning and stepped out with a towel around his waist.

He almost collided with Anastasia Dubinina, who wore a bathrobe and carried a towel. She didn't smile as he said good morning and excuse me, and when he cleared the door, she slipped in and quickly shut the door.

Stiletto dressed in his room and went out to the living room, where Rina and her daughter sat on the couch with breakfast and Ravkin handed him a mug of tea.

"I have news," Ravkin said.

Stiletto joined him at a wobbly table near the

kitchen area, where instant oatmeal was cooking on the hotplate. The scent of maple filled the room. Ravkin's laptop computer sat on the table.

"One of my contacts reported back. We might have a lead on Vlad."

Stiletto sipped his tea. English Breakfast, dark and very heavy. "Where?"

Ravkin opened an email and Stiletto examined the Cyrillic, but couldn't decipher the words. It was a short email, only a few lines.

"From one of my people at FSB," Ravkin said. "I asked who might be a likely candidate for holding Vlad, and he came back with one name."

"Which is?"

Ravkin used the touchpad to highlight the name. "Leonid Pushkin. He's a mid-level boss, but he has family connections in oil and farming. He could have squirreled away a high-value individual like Vlad."

Stiletto drank some tea while Ravkin dished up oatmeal.

"I passed Anastasia in the hallway," Scott said. "Does she ever smile?"

"She used to," Ravkin replied.

"What happened?"

"What always happens in our line of work?

The man she was seeing got killed in the line of duty."

"How?"

"Undercover in the Mob."

They finished breakfast, and Stiletto asked to see a picture of Pushkin and whatever else Ravkin could access. A simple internet search turned up a picture and details on Pushkin's only alleged source of income, a dance club called Pulse. News stories detailed renovations and the grand opening —lots of neon, fancy outfits, and smiling faces. Pushkin had two gold teeth.

"We will pay Mr. Pushkin a visit," Scott said, "and ask him a few questions."

Out the corner of his eye, Stiletto saw Rina watching them while Xenia laughed at a cartoon.

"I'll need to stay here," Ravkin said. "You and Anastasia can go."

"Why can't *she* stay? I don't like the idea of doing this sort of thing with somebody who might go a little too far."

"Oh, she will," Ravkin agreed. "But she needs to get out of this place more than I do. She'll go, as you Americans say, bonkers before the rest of us."

"All right," Scott said. He scooped the last of

the oatmeal into his mouth. "Make sure she's OK with it. How are we fixed for weapons?"

"You have your pistol."

"I was thinking of something that could provide a little more persuasion should the need arise."

Ravkin smiled, and there was a gleam in his eye. "I think I have exactly what you need."

ANASTASIA OPENED the bathroom door a crack to let out the steam and wiped the mirror with her towel. She wore her robe, belted tight, and her hair was still wet. The eyes that looked back at her in the mirror showed the strain she felt inside, the dark circles under them not helping her appearance one bit. She was glad for the shower, though. Small comforts mattered.

She thought about the American. He wasn't arrogant, and seemed genuinely interested in helping. She wondered if his devotion to Glinkov might mean she and Ravkin were expendable, but dismissed that thought as quickly as it came. Whoever Ravkin was working for wanted all of them out; that was why they had helped Stiletto get into Russia. All backs would get scratched. The only problem was, she didn't know what she would do outside of Russia, or where she would go.

How had Glinkov and Stiletto met? What had made Vlad contact him? Obviously, he had his good points. She decided to try to find out what they were. There was no reason to keep being sour about the situation when there might be some light at the end of the tunnel.

She hated to be leaving Russia by herself.

There was a knock on the cracked door, and Anastasia saw Xenia standing in the gap with wide eyes.

"Need the bathroom, honey?"

The girl nodded twice sharply.

Anastasia gave her robe's belt a reassuring tug, grabbed her wet towel, and changed places with the girl. Back in her room, she dried her hair and dressed and wandered out to join the others. She skipped the oatmeal, peeling a banana instead. More small comforts—fresh fruit was something she couldn't live without.

Ravkin and Stiletto invited her to the table, where they talked over the information in the email and went over a plan of action.

When Stiletto asked, "What about those weapons we talked about?" Anastasia was as curious as the American when Ravkin stood up and told them to follow him.

Down the hall in his bedroom, Ravkin tossed aside a throw rug and opened a trapdoor. The hidden compartment was dusty, and some of it drifted into the room. Anastasia covered her mouth, and Stiletto turned away to cough.

Ravkin lifted out a long, rectangular Pelican case, undid the clasp on the front, and lifted the lid.

"If you can't do it with what's in here," he said, "you shouldn't try."

Stiletto whistled, and Anastasia approached almost reverently. Several weapons with assorted ammunition filled the foam case. Scott lifted out a SEA Bears Bark 20-gauge sawed-off double-barreled shotgun. It had twin triggers with concealed hammers. The barrels were scratched and the wooden grip was a little rough, but it looked good enough to use. A fully-automatic Glock-17C caught his eye, along with an AR-type MK18 MOD0 .223 short-barrel submachine gun, full auto. Anastasia lifted out a Dakota Tactical D54R-N A3, which resembled a compact HK MP5K. Stiletto put the shotgun down and said, "All US weapons."

"From our mutual friends."

Stiletto scanned the rest of the case: suppressors, shotgun shells, and loaded mags. A heck of a lot more than his .45 pistol.

"Well, I guess we'll take one or two things, all right?"

Anastasia snapped the breech of the D54R closed. "I get this one."

Ravkin said, "Pushkin will never know what hit him."

Anastasia drove Ravkin's car, and Stiletto sat in the passenger seat wearing a long overcoat. He had the sawed-off shotgun slung under one arm and the short-barreled MK18 MOD0 under the other. The .45 rode behind his back, but he doubted he'd even need that.

Anastasia's slender fingers held the wheel loosely as they moved through the late-night traffic. It had been a long day at the safehouse, the routine broken only by quick strolls around the block for fresh air. Glinkov's daughter was having the hardest time. Her mother now worried that she was talking less and less for reasons she didn't understand.

They stopped at a traffic light.

"How do you know Vlad?" she asked.

"He helped us out on a few joint missions," Stiletto said. He dared not mention the information Vlad had covertly passed to the US. "One of them took place here in Russia."

"When?"

"About a year ago, maybe. I was looking for some neo-Nazis, and they decided to hide here."

Anastasia laughed. "I suppose they could have done something more stupid than that."

"They did."

"Oh?"

"They killed a bunch of our people and got away."

"Now I remember," she said. "We had many bad days after that. You got them all?"

"Every last one."

Anastasia pressed the gas pedal as the light changed and Stiletto noticed something he hadn't seen since meeting the woman—she smiled. It was a half-smile, one of satisfaction at knowing that an enemy had been removed from existence. Scott thought maybe they could actually get along now.

"Did Ravkin tell you about me?" she asked.

Traffic crept along.

"Couple things," Scott said.

"Like what?"

"You lost a lover to the Mob. He was undercover."

"Yes." Her voice softened. "The night he died, we had an argument about whether or not we were going to get married. He wanted to, but I didn't. We never finished talking about it."

She drove some more.

"What happened to the gang that did it?"

"They're gone. Every last one."

"You?"

"Me and some others."

"Ravkin?"

"All he did was find them for us."

Stiletto said nothing.

"Here we are," she announced.

They passed the neon-fronted club, the word PULSE flashing on and off. Anastasia turned a corner and found an open curb space. There was barely enough room, but she wedged the sedan into the spot and they exited the car.

She wore a long coat too, the sleeves too long for her arms. The cuffs were rolled back. She carried the full-auto Glock-17C and the Dakota

Tactical D54R, but no bulges showed under either of their coats.

Scott followed Anastasia across the street, and she pushed through the cluster of young people on the sidewalk to get to the front door. No line, no doorman with a list. Stiletto frowned. He'd have expected that. He followed in her wake, his eyes scanning for threats. He spotted a few not-so-hidden cameras, but no muscle. The wide alcove of the entrance felt like daytime; bright lights, radiating body heat, music thumping, and fresh air mixed with cigarette smoke and laughter.

Inside, Scott had another surprise waiting.

Pulse was a karaoke club, with a trio of inebriated patrons on a small stage belting out some sort of Russia pop song off-key.

Even with that, it wasn't the rowdy dance place he'd expected. Plush couches sat against the left-side walls, and the bar occupied the right side. The center of the club was less of a dance floor and more of a dining area with tables and chairs, the tables polished glass. The floor had a black-and-white zigzag pattern. Track lighting provided plenty of illumination, and big speakers hung from the ceiling. There was no way to not hear the singers or the music. The floor vibrated with the bass.

Stiletto let out a sigh. He hated karaoke. But while he grumbled, he noticed a set of stairs beside the stage that led to a second floor.

"Pushkin's office is up those steps," Anastasia told him.

"This place was his idea?"

"He's a frustrated performer."

They were not totally out of place with their long overcoats. The attire of most customers was business casual or semi-formal, and not everybody was watching the singers.

It was all so Americanized that Stiletto decided that had it not been for the language, he might be in New York City.

"Stop gawking," Anastasia said. She started forward, waving off a hostess who was about to ask if they wanted a table. Stiletto followed her across the zigzag floor to the stairs.

They went up the steps. The landing and short hallway above them were lit brightly and a lone guard stood at the hallway entrance, out of sight of patrons below. He stepped forward as Anastasia cleared the final step.

"Can't come up here."

She stepped to one side as Stiletto slipped the sawed-off from under his coat and bashed the guard on the side of the head. The floor shook when he hit the carpet. Anastasia drew the suppressor-fitted Dakota Tactical and advanced down the hall to a door at the end, then kicked it open. Stiletto followed her through.

"What is this?" shouted the man behind the desk. He wore a dark suit, and had a full head of hair despite the wrinkles on his face and pronounced jowls. He turned a paler shade of white when he saw the gaping end of the shotgun. Anastasia swept the room with the muzzle of her weapon, but there were no other guards to deal with.

"Where is Glinkov?" Stiletto demanded.

"You're American?"

Anastasia turned her weapon on Pushkin and fired once. The bullet chugged quietly out of the muzzle, destroying the computer monitor on Pushkin's desktop. It sparked and flung sharp pieces of debris everywhere, and Pushkin threw up an arm to shield his face. He lowered his arm and looked incredulous.

"What is the meaning of this? Tell me!"

"Vlad Glinkov," Stiletto said.

"What about him?"

"Where is he?"

"Why should I tell you?"

"Because her next round goes through your head."

"Then how will I answer your question?"

Anastasia fired again. This time Pushkin screamed as the bullet punched through his right shoulder and he clumsily fell out of the chair. Anastasia dragged Pushkin by his shirt collar, the fabric ripping in the process, onto the middle of the floor.

The big Russian made whimpering noises as his eyes shifted between the two people standing over him.

"I meant the round after that," Scott Stiletto said.

"Why do you care about Glinkov?" Pushkin said through the pain filling his face. "Are you traitors too?"

Scott knelt beside the man. "Tell me where he is. Otherwise—"

Pushkin spat at Scott, who wiped his face, then rose. "Well, I guess we'll have to kill him."

Anastasia grinned and lifted her weapon.

"Wait!"

Anastasia lowered her weapon.

Pushkin gasped, sweat beading his forehead. A trickle ran down the side of his face as he looked up at Scott.

"There's an oil refinery," Pushkin began. He talked for two minutes, ending with, "That's all I know."

"He's still alive?"

"I think so. If he wasn't, they would not have consulted with me. May I have an ambulance now?"

Anastasia said, "No," and raised her weapon once more. Stiletto jumped back as the top of Pushkin's head popped like a dropped watermelon, but the cuffs of his pants and shoes couldn't avoid the spatter of blood.

Anastasia's face remained stoic.

CHAPTER 10

Anastasia powered into traffic as Stiletto checked their back.

"There's a lot to say for noise covering your exit," he said. Only normal traffic was behind them, the neon flash of Pulse fading in the distance. And then—

"Make a few extra turns," Scott said. There was one car, the make of which he couldn't tell in the glare of the headlamps, aggressively weaving through lanes. The car closed the distance quickly.

Anastasia turned onto Leningradsky Avenue and the engine grumbled as she pressed the accelerator, weaving through cars and honking, Stiletto gripping his seat to keep from being jostled. The headlamps of the unknown car stayed with them, now only a few cars back.

"Do we have a tail?" she said.

"For sure."

Stiletto faced forward, buckled up, and loosened the sawed-off shotgun. He placed it in his lap.

"I see them," Anastasia said after a quick glance in the rearview mirror.

Stiletto held his breath for a moment, then let it out. Not a clean getaway after all. It had been too easy up in the office, the noise of the club drowning out any sign of their activity and the crowd outside adding more cover as they made their way back to the car, but now the enemy was on their tail. There might be no avoiding a street fight.

He looked forward. Streetlights flashed past, and the storefronts were a blur. Anastasia powered through a yellow light.

"That car just turned off," she said.

Scott looked back. There were plenty of other cars.

"They're going to try to box us in."

Scott lurched as Anastasia made a sharp right turn, then sat forward again.

"They can't do that if they can't catch up," she said. "What's the plan if they do?"

"Shoot our way out."

"Is that the best you can do?"

"Do you have another idea?"

"The passages."

"What?"

"Tunnels under the street."

The cabin brightened as a car behind them got right on their bumper, high beams unmerciful. Scott grabbed the shotgun, resting his finger on the trigger.

Another sharp turn onto Butyrskaya. The car sped onward, the street less crowded as the buildings turned to closed offices and warehouses. Stiletto spotted signs for the Savyolovsky railway station ahead

Anastasia let out a curse and slammed on the brakes, and Stiletto strained against the seatbelt. A car blasted out of an alley ahead and screeched to a stop in front of them. Anastasia threw the car into Park and leaped out of the car, Stiletto behind her. Other doors opened and closed around him. Horns blared, and people yelled. Lying on his side with the greasy blacktop beneath him, Stiletto aimed the shotgun at the wheel of the car in front of them and let off a barrel. The roar shook the night and the front right tire exploded, sending shrapnel and bits of rubber everywhere. Men yelled and screamed as Stiletto rolled to his feet and ran around the front of the car. Anastasia waited near the mouth of an alley. Scott almost stopped when he heard somebody call his name, but he kept going.

Anastasia turned and started running as Scott neared. He reached the alley, then looked back. Two men from both cars converged, three of them with drawn guns. The fourth man held no weapon and continued calling Scott's name. The street lamps highlighted him perfectly.

David McNeil.

Dammit!

Scott turned and ran after Anastasia. The Mafia wasn't after them. This wasn't related to Pushkin.

The CIA had found him.

STILETTO'S BOOTS pounded the pavement as he stayed behind Anastasia, trusting her instincts to get them out of the area.

And McNeil was behind him, sent by General Ike, no doubt, to try to reel him in. He didn't blame the general. One had to keep up appearances. It was Scott's job to avoid capture, however. Nothing good would come of him being brought home, and he doubted the Trust would in any way step in.

They reached the street at the other end of the alley and kept running along the sidewalk, dodging pedestrians who expressed various levels of vitriol at being jostled by the sprinting couple. Anastasia cut across the street, Stiletto shooting a glance back as he followed. McNeil and his crew had cleared the alley, but he was missing two. They were probably back in the undamaged car, trying to circle around for an interception.

Fenced-off construction zones along the street funneled traffic into one lane. Scott felt mildly disoriented by the blaze of bright headlamps, the nighttime darkness, and the unfamiliar territory, and he stayed close to Anastasia, no longer looking back. His lungs burned with the exertion. The sidewalk narrowed as part of a construction closure extended onto it. Anastasia powered through, knocking down one or two people, Stiletto leaping over one of the fallen. She turned a corner and ran into a parking lot.

Anastasia stopped and lifted a circular manhole. She shoved the cover to one side and started down the hole, Scott following, then pulling the cover back into place, his fingers almost getting crunched. He started down the ladder after Anastasia, who waited on a concrete walkway.

She ducked into an alcove to open another door with a key from her pocket, and the door squeaked open. Stiletto followed her, and she shut the door and bolted the lock. They stood in the dark. Scott took out his cell phone and shined a light around—a narrow tunnel indeed.

"It branches off from the sewer," she said. "We can follow it back to the streets near the safehouse."

She spoke while panting, Stiletto catching his breath as well.

"That wasn't the Mafia," he told her.

"Who were they then?"

"My people. Americans. The CIA."

"Why is the CIA after you?"

"Because I'm not supposed to be here," he said.

"I thought— Then why *are* you here?"

"Vlad is my friend. I don't have many."

She watched him blankly, still breathing hard. Finally, she said, "Come on," and led the way once again.

McNeil gave up the pursuit once witnesses said

the people he pursued had gone down the manhole.

They were already pushing it after Stiletto's shotgun blast. If the Russians caught them worming around underground, there'd be hell to pay.

He reunited with the rest of his crew in the good car and went back to the embassy. He'd have to report the shooting and the damaged car, and the embassy would have to deal with the cops on that one and work out some sort of cover story.

McNeil stewed all the way back.

In the embassy cafeteria, he sat quietly at a corner table, letting a cup of coffee get cold.

He looked up when Joe Wilcox, his contact at the embassy, dropped into the unoccupied chair opposite him.

"Staking out Pushkin was a good idea," Wilcox said. "Do you have any other ideas?"

"Bring in Pushkin. They went there for a reason."

"We can't."

"Why?"

"Pushkin was shot in the head. The cops are looking for a man and a woman, and they know the man is American. They didn't exactly hide their faces, and they left a guard alive."

McNeil shook his head.

"Stiletto is in more trouble than he realizes," Wilcox said.

ANASTASIA LED them through a maze of tunnels, Stiletto losing any sense of where they were many times. The rumbles of car engines and street traffic were sometimes audible through the concrete above. Presently she stopped at a ladder, climbed to the top, and popped open another manhole. After a look around, she slid the lid back and climbed up to the street, and Stiletto followed. They made a long sprint up two blocks before finally reaching the safehouse, where a nervous Ravkin greeted them and explained that the cops were hunting them for Pushkin's murder, and that they had his car. That meant he was a suspect too.

Stiletto explained the circumstances of leaving the car but had nothing to say about Pushkin. Anastasia handled that, but her flippant answer didn't satisfy Ravkin. Before an argument could start, Stiletto told Ravkin what Pushkin had revealed.

"The mob is using an oil refinery near Leninsky Avenue near the Moskva River as a hide-out. Glinkov is being kept there."

Ravkin forgot about Anastasia and went to his laptop. He typed hurriedly and clicked on a picture of the refinery.

Ravkin said, "I'm afraid that's never been on our radar as a place for them to use."

"We don't know how old the information is," Scott said, "so Vlad might not be there anymore. But the security is armed, it's hard to get in and out of, and nobody would come looking there."

Ravkin agreed.

"Let's go knock on the front door."

Rina Glinkov came over from the couch. "What about us?"

"You'll be safe here," Ravkin assured her.

The little girl joined her mother and wrapped both arms around her left leg. She looked at Scott, Anastasia, and Ravkin around her mother's thigh.

"Are you going to bring back my daddy?"

None of them could muster an immediate answer, then Scott thought back to another child who had asked him a similar question not very long ago.

He said, "We'll bring him back, honey."

Xenia smiled.

THE BRIGHT LIGHTS of the refinery blazed into a narrow portable building on the west end of the property, so Rostov had ordered heavy drapes put over the windows. The light still broke through the gaps around the edges, giving the light an eclipse effect.

He hadn't wanted to remain in charge of the detail holding Vladimir Glinkov prisoner, but orders were orders.

The building had been brought onto the property specifically for the purposes of using it as a jail. They had Glinkov chained to the wall, naked except for a t-shirt now stained with sweat and blood. He lay slumped against the wall and half on the floor, unconscious, his breathing slow. There was still plenty of information to get out of him, Rostov's bosses and the government believed, so they didn't want to dump him in the river yet.

But to Rostov, the chance of a rebel counterattack was all too real. He'd asked for twenty men, and his bosses had laughed. At the refinery? Somebody will notice. You can have ten men; that should be more than enough. His crew had spread out around the refinery wearing appropriate uniforms and badges, and so far, there had been no trouble. If the government had rounded up all of the coup suspects, there would be no more need for Glinkov.

But as he sat behind a desk at the far end of the portable building shuffling a deck of cards for a game of solitaire, he reflected that not only did he have his orders, but he also didn't make the decisions.

However, he'd be fully in charge of his destiny once he retired.

When the alarm went off, he dropped the cards and ran to the door. Two guards cradling short-barreled AKs stood at the ready.

"What's happening?" Rostov asked.

One of the guards had a radio set in his ear. "I can't raise the front gate, sir."

"Send somebody to look."

THE GATE of the refinery was right off Leningradsky Avenue. The Moskva River was a backdrop, with more city lights across the water. The guard shack was brightly lit and the automatic gate was firmly closed, and as he approached, Stiletto decided the opening mechanism was most likely on the panel on the guard shack. The guard looked up at him as he came within six feet.

The man stepped out with a hand up. "Turn around. It's after working hours."

Stiletto dragged the shotgun from the pocket of his overcoat and smashed the guard on the side of the head, but the man didn't drop. He leaned to one side, caught his balance, and looked angrily at Scott. He let out a curse as he swung in return. Stiletto ducked the fist and snapped a leg out to kick the guard in the stomach. The man doubled over but didn't fall, grabbing Scott's leg and twisting. Scott hit the ground hard on his side. The wind was knocked out of him, and he lost his grip on the weapon. The guard kicked him in the back, and Stiletto grabbed his weapon and started to turn as the guard ran back to the shack and hit the alarm button.

The wailing Klaxon filled the night, and the shotgun boomed once. The guard went down in a spatter of blood, broken glass, and splintered wood. Once on his feet, Scott was quickly joined by Ravkin and Anastasia. Ravkin propped him up as Anastasia reached through the open guard shack and pressed the button on the panel that opened the gate.

"So much for quiet," Ravkin said.

Stiletto, gasping, only nodded. He dropped two more shells into the shotgun.

"They make you people out of solid rock or something?"

"How do you think we survive the winters?" Anastasia asked, heading through the open gate onto the property. She carried her Dakota Tactical D54R-N A3 like she'd had it since birth.

Stiletto and Ravkin followed, the trio quickly splitting up to take care of the individual tasks they'd worked out in the car.

The refinery was immense. The sprawling complex contained a set of buildings off to one side, and a mass of pipes, storage containers, pumping units, and tanks on the other. The pipes were intertwined like multiple spiderwebs and lit up by bright lamps that made it feel like daylight. The glare of the lights clashed against the dark background of the night sky.

Stiletto put away the shotgun and brought up the MK18 submachine gun. His job was to search the buildings for any sign of Glinkov, and with the alarm blaring, they had to be quick. Enemy forces would be all over, and the alarm would also signal cops and federal agents.

Stiletto dropped to one knee beside an obviously empty building, the door padlocked. He caught his breath and looked around. Another building sat about twenty yards ahead, but that looked empty too. He pushed on, clearing the open distance quickly, then reached a corner and tried to peer through a window. It was an office of some sort with spotless desks and obvious signs of everyday use, but nothing was in use now. Stiletto moved along the length of the building to the far corner and spotted the portable.

Well, duh. This one had two guards out front. There were other gunmen racing from another nearby building to the center of the refinery, all armed with Kalashnikovs, but the two gunmen by the portable building did not move, although they sure looked antsy enough and ready to do so.

Stiletto needed to get past those two guards. He knew Vlad was inside. Obviously alive, or why bother with the shooters? But he also couldn't engage them yet. The walls of the portable wouldn't stop any stray .223 rounds from the MK18. Accidentally killing Vlad wasn't an option.

He'd have to explain what happened to Xenia, and she wouldn't understand.

He looked around for another way to approach the building without attacking it head-on.

RAVKIN WOVE through the mass of pipes and pumps, ducking the low ones and stopping when he came to the metal cabinet he was looking for.

He took out the full-auto Glock-17C and smashed the padlock holding the protective doors closed, opened them, and briefly examined the switches and dials within. The dials all showed green, and the humming pumps around him all emitted a low drone. He breathed hard from running, but he knew what to press and started hitting the cooling fan switches. The fans spinning on the exterior of the larger tanks slowed to a stop but the pumps kept going, oil in various stages of refinement flowing but the needles showing the temperature of said fluid rising rapidly. The needle moved from green to yellow, then into the red and red cherry lights began flashing. More alarms joined the original klaxon, and Ravkin looked up to see a swarm of armed men closing in on him. He jerked out the Glock and steadied his arm against the side of the cabinet.

He wanted to keep them occupied and away from Anastasia, and especially Stiletto. A line of flame spat from the Glock, a controlled three-round burst. The gunners scattered, bullets ricocheting off pipes and creating a danger as they continued to bounce from pipe to pipe, the whine of the slugs barely audible over the new alarm. Ravkin fired another burst.

Return fire came his way, striking the cabinet and sending sparks flying, black smoke coming from the back. The cooling fans stopped completely, but the alarm continued. Ravkin ran.

ANASTASIA SQUATTED behind a cooling cylinder about five inches off the ground and twelve feet in length. The outside of the cylinder was very hot. A thin pipe went in one end and out the other.

She braced the Dakota Tactical on the top, aiming for the troops chasing Ravkin. Her first burst brought down a rear straggler, and her second clipped the shoulder of a man up front. Others turned her way and opened fire, and Anastasia ducked. She fired from underneath the cylinder, but none of her shots connected as the gunners sought cover among the myriad of pipes.

She moved right, staying low, her submachine gun held high.

She saw him fire at the gunners as he moved and she sprayed rounds their way too. Their return fire was erratic, and none of the rounds came particularly closer to her.

The alarm continued, pounding her eardrums, and the red cherry lights continued flashing. She wasn't sure what Ravkin had done or how long until things reached critical mass, but she wanted to be out of there before it happened.

Ravkin dropped behind cover and sprayed rounds while Anastasia broke off from his trail and advanced toward the shooters, ducking and dodging pipes. As she went by one, a valve snapped, the break sounding like a gunshot, and a jet of steam blasted at the back of her head. She lunged forward, hitting the ground hard. Gunners looked her way and fired, the ricochets pounding around her and one smacking into the ground inches from her face. She raised her SMG and fired back, knocking down one gunner as his buddies advanced toward Ravkin.

Anastasia took a shot and another gunner dropped. She counted three still on their feet.

The three shooters poured fire at Ravkin as she moved closer, then her SMG spat flame. One shooter down, two left. One turned her way, and she dropped as more ricochets pelted the pipes, letting out a scream when one of the stray rounds smashed the action of her Dakota Tactical. The broken SMG fell from her stung fingers and she hit the ground. They must have thought she was out for good because they didn't bother to come check. Their fire intensified.

She had no handgun. Staying flat, she scrambled along the ground, breaking into a run toward one of the dead gunners about ten yards away. She scooped up his Kalashnikov and a spare magazine and charged back to her last position.

She slammed to a stop against a vertical pipe, shouldering the AK and aiming at the backs of the gunmen. As she squeezed the trigger, one of them hit Ravkin. Ravkin rose a little too high, and the salvo from his Glock cut off as AK rounds stitched through him. He let out a clipped yell, the slugs opening small red holes across his chest and exploding out the back. Ravkin's body dropped, and Anastasia screamed. Her first blast split open the back of one shooter, but the other took off running. She fired, and the burst clipped his heels but didn't bring him down.

Anastasia pounded after him, leaping over the other gunners' bodies and making a sharp left turn down a narrow walkway. More pipes and tanks surrounded her. She shifted slightly and powered up a flight of steps, sprinting along a long catwalk, the last gunner right ahead and checking over his shoulder. He stopped with a confused look on his face, then Anastasia yelled out a curse. The man looked up, and Anastasia's burst took off the top of his head.

She collapsed to her knees, breathless. The alarm was still blaring, and more gunfire crackled far behind her.

She reloaded and ran back down the steps.

They couldn't get Scott too.

STILETTO BROKE LEFT, staying close to the empty buildings and using the shadows for cover. He gripped the MK18 in both hands.

His boots scuffed on the concrete as he moved, and then he tripped on a raised section of the concrete. He fell headlong and landed hard with a grunt, MK18 flying out of his hands. It slid across the ground.

One of the guards at the portable building shined a flashlight that might as well have been a spotlight, and the beam landed right on him. Somebody shouted and two shots popped but Scott was already moving, rolling left and deeper into the shadows. The long coat got tangled around him, but he managed to get to his feet and toss the coat away. The light beam danced as the guard converged alone, his mate remaining by the portable.

Stiletto grabbed for the .45 under his arm, but his hand closed on an empty holster. He scanned the ground frantically as the guard closed the distance, but saw no sign of his Colt. It must have slipped out while he was rolling.

Stiletto retreated deeper into the shadows, his back against the building's wall. The shotgun under his right arm remained in place, and he grabbed it with his left hand. Breaking the action, he took out the shell he'd fired at the shack and replaced it. He closed the action as the guard shined the light again and brought up his AK, and Stiletto raised the shotgun at the same time. He fired first, both barrels, the blast almost louder than the alarm, and the guard's chest split open. Stiletto crouched, spotting the .45 and grabbing it. He scooped up the guard's flashlight and started for the portable. When he was close enough and the remaining guard called out a name, Scott blinded him with the flash and fired a .45 slug through his head. Blood and bits of bone created a kaleidoscope-like pattern on the wall as his body thudded on the ground.

Stiletto yelled in Russian, and the door swung open and another man came out holding a pistol. Two shots from the .45 sent him tumbling down the steps. The man's body stopped at Scott's feet.

Stiletto ran up the steps and into the building, swinging the .45 left and right and stopping at the body chained to the wall. The man's eyes connected with Stiletto's.

Vladimir Glinkov smiled, although he was missing a few teeth and his upper body was full of welts and cuts.

But he was alive.

Stiletto holstered the .45 and took out a pocket knife. He started sawing at Glinkov's ropes.

"My family?"

"Safe. Ravkin and Anastasia are with me."

"I failed," Glinkov moaned. "I couldn't hold out."

The ropes snapped, and Stiletto helped the injured man to his feet. He leaned heavily against Scott.

"Later," Stiletto said. "We gotta get out of here."

Glinkov tried to walk and limped at first, but gritted his teeth and remained upright, almost falling down the steps and taking Stiletto with him. Another figure ran toward them from the shadows and Stiletto started to lift the .45, but let off the trigger once he recognized Anastasia.

"Vlad!"

She ran to assist, and they started for the gate.

"Ravkin's dead," she told them.

"Let's get out of here, Ana," Stiletto said, but Glinkov suddenly felt heavier.

"I can walk," the injured man said, and Stiletto let him go. He kept up as they moved faster toward the gate.

Sirens wailed. Half a dozen police cars with flashing cherry lights pulled up at the gate, several continuing onto the property while two stayed at the shack.

Anastasia called, "The river's behind us!"

"Vlad, can you run?"

"If I have too."

Anastasia steered them left, and Stiletto stayed behind Vlad. The man jogged steadily, but Scott saw him wincing and breathing hard.

But they weren't faster than the police cars. Two stopped in a wedge behind them while another pair screeched to a halt in front of them. All three stopped short. Cops jumped out with handguns leveled and started shouting.

Stiletto had started to say something when Anastasia raised her Kalashnikov and opened fire.

CHAPTER 11

Anastasia's heart sank as the cars surrounded them. She skidded to a stop, and there was only one thought in her mind. She would not surrender. She'd get out of Russia or die trying.

She lifted the AK as the cops in front started shouting. Flame blazed from the muzzle as she raked the cop cars, one of the cops falling with blood bursting from the holes across his chest.

"Run!" she yelled, turning to the cops behind her and firing some more. Another cop fell, and one fired back.

Stiletto grabbed Glinkov's left arm and pulled him along, the pair running around the cars blocking them and deeper into the property. Scott focused on the darkness ahead, knowing the perimeter fence lay a hair beyond.

He looked back and saw Anastasia fall, her AK chattering skyward as she collapsed. He let out a curse.

"Don't look back, Vlad!"

They ran on, reaching the shadows, then the whipping rotor blades of a chopper drowned out the alarm. The helicopter passed low over the refinery, the forward-mounted spotlight shining on the ground. It landed on them and stayed there as they kept running. Scott raised the .45 and fired until the magazine locked back, but the chopper remained, tracking them closely. Glinkov fell, Stiletto trying to catch him and falling with him. He looked back. The cops who'd stopped at the gate had powered through and were heading straight for them.

Stiletto fished a spare magazine from the pouch on his belt and slapped it home, about to raise it toward the chopper once again when the refinery finally reached critical mass.

The ground shook as the first explosion went off, and when the fireball burst from the center, it engulfed everything in its path: pipes, tanks, and all of it, secondary explosions mixing with the first. Stiletto and Glinkov raised their arms to shield their faces and the chopper wavered, tipping from side to side. The pilot was forced to pull up and fly away before the shockwave knocked him out of the sky.

"Up, up, up!" Stiletto shouted, grabbing Glinkov, and they continued toward the fence. The heat from the blast touched Scott's back, but the fence was finally in sight. Glinkov crashed against the chain link, clamping both hands and trying to climb, but he let out a breath and collapsed.

Stiletto looked up the length of the fence to the barbed wire on top.

"Vlad, this is going to hurt."

"Already does."

"Step on my back."

Stiletto dropped to his hands and knees. The flames raged beyond. The glare of the blaze lit the night.

Glinkov placed one shaking foot on Stiletto's back and grasped the fence. He started pulling himself up and let out a cry of pain, but he didn't stop. He moved his hands and feet and reached the barbed wire and rolled over, tearing his clothes on the barbs, to climb down the other side.

Stiletto jumped up, scaled the fence quickly, and dropped beside his friend. "Let's go!"

Vlad Glinkov rose slowly but stayed on Stiletto's heels. The cold river lay only twenty yards ahead. They moved quickly across the ground, reaching the shore and splashing into the water. It looked like a million miles to the other side and, worse, the ice-cold water sliced through them, numbing in its intensity. Glinkov almost slid beneath the surface when they reached the deep part in the middle and Stiletto moved up beside him, throwing an arm around his back and pulling him close. Stiletto continued stroking, shivering and breathing hard, but the other side of the river still seemed miles away. Vlad kept going, kicking with his legs and swinging his left arm in an arc, propelling them forward. Presently they reached the edge and crawled out of the water, Glinkov rolling onto his back, still gasping, Stiletto stayed on hands and knees and coughed till his lungs hurt. He dropped onto his back and looked across the water at the blazing refinery on the other side.

They were away, but he'd left two allies behind. One of them had the bargaining chip he sorely needed to get them back to the US in one piece.

"There was nothing we could do, Scott," Glinkov said, his voice raspy.

"But we can't stay here," Stiletto said, forcing himself to his feet. His felt for his gun, took it out of his belt, and shook out some water.

Glinkov raised a hand, and Scott helped him to his feet. Vlad's skin was cold to the touch, and the man was already shivering. Stiletto couldn't hide his shaking either. They needed to get warm fast, and no mistake.

"We'll have to find a car to hijack," he said. "We're racking up all kinds of charges."

"Where are we going?"

"Safehouse first," Stiletto said, "and then we'll head to the embassy."

"What will they do?"

"Place us under house arrest," Stiletto said. "Then they'll turn us over to the police, unless there's a miracle."

His mission had gone totally out of control—if he had ever had any control to begin with.

Glinkov blinked.

"Come on," Scott urged.

STILETTO AND GLINKOV walked along a dirt road.

The lights of homes lay ahead, but before that was the Otkrytiye Arena, the circular building dark and imposing but with a cluster of cars in the parking lot.

Stiletto and Glinkov crossed a quiet dirt access road and continued on pavement toward the arena. Stiletto was still cold and Glinkov shivered, his arms wrapped around his torso.

They stopped beside a storage building and Glinkov slumped against the wall, then lowered himself to the pavement, breathing hard and shaking.

Stiletto stood at the corner watching the cars, only a handful for a small staff on duty. He looked at Glinkov, whose eyes were closed. Stiletto hoped the strain wasn't making his injuries worse. He had to act fast but not recklessly. He swallowed hard, his throat dry, and looked at the cars again. *Come on, somebody exit the building.* The glow of the refinery fire continued to light the night.

Finally, a side door opened and a lone man carrying a lunchbox exited. A potential weapon, Scott thought, as he told Glinkov to stay put and started for the lot with the .45 in his right fist.

He reached the man as he transferred the

lunchbox to his left hand, keys jingling in his right as he inserted them into the door lock.

Stiletto did not want the man to yell, swing the lunch box, or cause trouble, but if the man was as hard-headed as the gate guard, there'd be trouble no matter what.

Stiletto swung the pistol and connected solidly with the man's head.

The man's legs collapsed under him and Scott lunged to catch him, lowering him to the ground. He was out cold but breathing steadily, and he'd have one heck of a lump on his head. Stiletto gave the keys a twist to finish unlocking the door and jumped behind the wheel. It was an older car with a stick shift, and he jammed the stick into first and raced back to Glinkov.

The Russian's eyes widened as Stiletto climbed out and helped him to his feet. To Scott, he seemed to have more energy, thanks to the vehicle and the hope it provided, and Stiletto loaded him into the passenger seat and slid back behind the wheel.

He checked before they drove off: they had half a tank of gas. Stiletto turned the heat on full blast, and hot air filled the interior.

"I can't believe we made it," Glinkov said.

Stiletto made no reply as he executed a few

turns, the streets mostly empty, an odd glow from the refinery fire filling the night sky.

They were going back to the safehouse minus two, and no promises about what would happen next.

SCOTT LEFT the stolen car several blocks from the safehouse and he and Glinkov walked the rest of the way, both having warmed up to the point where they weren't shivering any longer.

Stiletto punched in the code for the safehouse door and led Glinkov inside. His wife and daughter sat on the couch, huddled together. She turned when the door opened, eyes wide, and gasped.

Scott could only stand back while wife embraced husband and the little girl joined them, all three hugging and crying. Stiletto went down the hall to a bedroom and took out his satellite phone. He dialed.

"Yes?" Number One's deep baritone came over the connection.

"It's Stiletto."

"You've made quite a bit of noise, Mr. Stiletto."

"Come get us. I have Glinkov, but we lost Ravkin and Anastasia."

"Unfortunate. Where are you?"

Scott hesitated, but he saw no other way than to reveal the location. He did.

"I'll have a recovery team there in fifteen minutes."

"How—" Scott didn't finish the question. The connection had ended.

Stiletto put the phone away and sorted through Ravkin's clothes, his heart heavy at the loss of him and Anastasia—two good people who had only wanted what was best for their country. But they had gone down fighting, and that was the only way it could have happened. Anything less would have been an insult.

Ravkin and Glinkov were almost the same size, and he brought the other man several choices and told him to get cleaned up in the shower because their extraction team was on the way. Glinkov kissed his family again and hurried down the hall.

Rina looked at Scott with watery eyes, and Xenia rushed forward and grabbed Stiletto around the left leg.

Neither needed to say thank you.

. . .

THE TRANSPORT VAN collected Stiletto and the Glinkovs on schedule and without incident. The group sat in the back of the van as they traveled through Moscow streets and out to the countryside, where they stopped at a private airfield under heavy guard. The guards, who all spoke Russian, shuffled the four from the van to a waiting Lear jet that took off within minutes of their arrival.

The plane was warm, and offered not only comfortable leather seats but plenty to eat and drink as well as satellite television for entertainment. The cabin's insulation reduced the roar of the jet engines to a dull throb. The pilots promised them a quick trip to Germany, where they would refuel and collect another pair of pilots who would fly them across the ocean to the US.

Vlad, still looking a little dazed but with clear eyes and his head up, cornered Scott in the galley as the agent poured a beer.

"I think we have a mutual friend," Glinkov said. Then he closed his eyes and winced.

"We gotta get you to a doctor."

"I'll live." Vlad opened his eyes. "Answer me."

Scott nodded. "This isn't a CIA plane."

"You've taken an incredible risk, Scott. I'm not sure I'm worth it."

"I don't want to hear that, Vlad. And it might have been for nothing anyway. I'm not sure what we'll do when we land. Ravkin had information stored in the cloud that would have helped get the heat off me and guaranteed safe passage for you, but without him, we're throwing ourselves on their mercy."

"You think they'll send us back?"

"I'm not sure what they'll do."

Rina came over. "No, wait. He gave me his password."

Stiletto gaped. "He *what*?"

"While you and Anastasia were at the night-club, he made me memorize his password."

Stiletto put the beer down and hurried to his seat, where there was a tablet computer bolted to the fuselage. He went through the retrieval process with Rina looking over his shoulder, and when the documents were open, he scrolled through each one carefully. Presently he sat back, stunned.

He glanced at Xenia, who sat in front of the television watching a cartoon. She had no idea of the real-life drama taking place behind her. If his sacrifice resulted in the little girl living a normal life in the US, he would consider the mission a success. However, the unanswered questions that lay ahead still gave him a twinge of doubt. The last thing he wanted was for her to be sent back to Russia to face the certain death of her father and perhaps her mother as well.

He smiled to show the confidence he didn't quite feel but the Glinkovs needed to see.

"I think we'll be fine after all," he told them.

CHAPTER 12

THE SHOWER FELT GOOD.

Stiletto turned off the water and stepped out of the steamy stall, dripping onto the blue shower mat, then drying off in front of the window, grateful for the foggy mirror that concealed his reflection. He didn't want to see his face. He didn't know what to think of the Moscow adventure, and he was scared about his future. Surely the CIA would want him out, but was the Trust a better option? Or was San Francisco? Had Ali changed her mind since their visit?

He pulled on clean clothes, provided by Number One. Their trip from Russia to Germany to Washington, DC had been smooth, a respite prior to the final battle between Scott and the

Agency bureaucrats. Glinkov's family was two floors below, and Glinkov himself was at the hospital being treated for his wounds. The physical ones, anyway. Guilt was going to crush Glinkov before anything else harmed him. Scott wanted to find a way to alleviate that if he could.

His cell phone sat on the writing table, and he had a text message waiting from the general.

DCI agrees. See you soon. Welcome home.

Stiletto had contacted the office and asked the general and DCI Webb to be at his hotel at four o'clock. It was two in the afternoon, so he had time to prepare.

IKE FLEMING HEARD the heavy footsteps of the guard behind him and Webb as they walked down the quiet hallway to Stiletto's hotel room.

They stopped short when they reached the door. It was already open a crack. The linebacker-looking guard pushed between them, drawing a pistol as he pushed the door open and took two steps inside.

Stiletto sat at the table, legs crossed, holding a bottle of beer. "You're late," he said.

The general and Webb entered and told the

guard to stand by the door. They approached Scott and stopped halfway into the room.

Fleming said, "Hello, Scott."

"General. Director Webb."

DCI Webb said, "This is highly irregular, Stiletto."

Scott gestured to the two empty chairs near the table. "Have a seat, and we'll talk."

"I don't think you're in a position to do much demanding," Webb shot back.

"I sense that you're upset with me, sir."

Webb and Fleming sat down. Fleming kept his mouth shut as Webb sounded off.

"You've broken Agency rules and regulations. You've violated the sovereign space of another country. The Russians want you for murder. There are all kinds of reasons I'm upset."

Stiletto placed the beer bottle near a thin stack of paper Fleming judged to be about a hundred pages. Webb kept his eyes on Scott.

"Have anything to say for yourself?"

"I deserve what I get, according to Agency disciplinary procedures," Scott said. "The murder charge isn't true. An accessory charge, maybe. The woman who killed Pushkin died at the refinery."

"That's a whole separate issue. I don't even

know where to start on taking you apart for that one."

"I don't care." Stiletto pushed the stack of papers their way. "This government will extend asylum to the Glinkov family or that information goes public."

"Are you blackmailing me?"

"Yes."

A red flush crawled up Webb's neck and he opened his mouth, but Fleming silenced him by placing a hand on his arm. "Sir, let's see what he has."

Webb's gaze snapped to Fleming. "Are you on his side?"

"I'm on the side of the truth, Carlton. Let's see the document."

Webb took the papers and started reading. Fleming didn't rush him. He glanced at Stiletto, who winked. Fleming shook his head. Stiletto took a drink of beer.

"This is outrageous," Webb exclaimed.

"It's all true, and that's a copy. The original files are stored on the cloud. I'm not kidding about that asylum."

"Mr. Stiletto," Webb said, handing the pages to Fleming, "as of this moment, you are no longer an employee of the CIA. We cannot allow your breach of protocol to go unpunished. Everybody's watching to see what I do."

"May I at least empty my desk?"

"I'll have somebody clear your desk and deliver your personal items."

"That's fine."

Webb frowned but said nothing more as Fleming read the opening pages. He whistled. The document detailed Vladimir's Putin's arrangement with the Russian Mafia to be his proxy in other nations. Activities included the murders of dissidents and those of other nationalities Putin deemed a threat to New Russia.

"This can't get out, Carlton," Fleming said.

"No kidding."

"Do I get what I want?" Scott asked.

"They'll be allowed to settle in the United States," Webb said. "On the condition that this information is destroyed and I never see you again."

"Can't promise either," Stiletto said. "I'm only getting started. Would either of you like a beer while we discuss this further?"

. . .

Stiletto stepped into the hospital room with the echo of a hallway announcement behind him.

Vlad Glinkov lay quietly in the bed staring at the wall, his eyes blank. He blinked and turned his head when he saw Scott.

"Hi," Scott said.

Glinkov nodded.

"So they beat the garbage out of you," Stiletto said, "and doped you up."

Glinkov stared past Scott.

"There's no way you could have beaten the drugs, Vlad. We all know that."

Glinkov only nodded.

"You and your family will be able to stay in the US," Scott told him. "Ravkin's information guarantees that. I've threatened to release it if the government doesn't cooperate."

A new voice. "Quite a bold move, Mr. Stiletto."

Scott turned to see Number One standing in the doorway. He was dressed in a dark suit with his vest buttoned tightly over his belly. He held a box covered with pink wrapping paper. Number One approached the bed.

"This is for your little girl, Vlad." He set the box on the bedside table.

Glinkov muttered his thanks.

"Has Scott told you he's been fired from the CIA?"

Glinkov blinked in surprise.

"Part of the deal," Scott explained.

"He shouldn't worry," Number One continued. "He has a bright future. You too, Vladimir."

Finally, Glinkov spoke clearly. "I don't see much of one."

"You didn't give up as much as you think," Number One said.

"They showed me the news."

"They showed you what they wanted you to see."

Glinkov frowned.

"Those news reports were propaganda for the public. Most of the anti-Putin cells were able to run or stay undercover and avoided the sweep. The thing is, Vlad, once my people got involved, we expanded the scope of the operations. Without your knowledge, of course. We recruited more people, sometimes deep within the government."

He turned to Stiletto. "That was how we got you out." Back to Vlad. "Most of the people arrested were criminals wanted by the FSB, gangsters and other kinds of criminals that our people used to make the dragnet look good to the Kremlin.

In other words, right now they're making people sweat who have no knowledge whatsoever of a coup."

"But the others—"

"Yes, those in your immediate network were compromised, but they are still alive. They are far too valuable to kill. We're making plans to recover as many as we can, one way or another. The only ones we lost were Dimitri and Anastasia."

Those names drove a spike through Stiletto's chest.

"You all knew the risks, Vlad. You have to be cold about this. About a lot of things. But none of this has been in vain."

Glinkov nodded.

"The coup will happen. Putin will fall."

Glinkov blinked and took a deep breath.

Rina and Xenia arrived. "We heard he's awake," Rina said. She and their daughter stepped up to the bed.

"I'll let your husband share the good news, Mrs. Glinkov," Number One said. "Mr. Stiletto and I need to have a private chat."

It was hard not to feel like he was caught up in a whirlwind when Number One was around,

Stiletto thought as he followed the older man out of the room.

I WASN'T KIDDING about your bright future, Mr. Stiletto."

They walked outside the hospital building and over to a garden with benches, but neither sat. Number One stopped in a shady spot, the leaves of a tree hanging above them. None of the leaves moved in the still afternoon air.

"I can't work for you full-time," Stiletto said.

"Why not?"

"I've decided to go freelance."

"I wasn't expecting that at all."

"I'll be available if and when you need me," Stiletto said, "but there are things nobody else will do that I need to give attention to."

"Well, then this chat will be short. However, I'm glad you'll be available, and we *will* need you, so we'll provide the retainer we spoke of. That will help you get started on your own, at least."

"Much appreciated."

"By the way, General Ike wants to see you. He's waiting on a bench near the Lincoln Memorial gift shop."

. . .

STILETTO FOUND the general munching popcorn.

Fleming sat beside the Lincoln Retail Refreshment and Gift Shop a stone's throw from the memorial, the side of the structure visible from the shop's outdoor seating area. A cluster of trees ahead stood between the shop and the reflecting pool. Tourists strolled around, but none made a lot of noise.

Stiletto sat next to his former boss.

"Nice day for a visit," the general said.

"I'm not sure what to call you anymore."

"'Ike' will be fine, Scott."

"Yes, sir."

The general laughed and offered Stiletto some popcorn. Scott took a handful.

"Your dismissal was not what I wanted," the general said.

"Couldn't be avoided. Webb was right. If I was the talk of the Agency, everybody was going to be watching to see what he did."

"What's your plan?"

Stiletto explained.

General Ike nodded. "Fair enough. Make sure you charge the numerical equivalent of a shit-ton if we ever come looking to hire you. It's only right you get something out of this organization."

"I appreciate what you did for me."

"I don't know what you're talking about."

"Of course, sir."

"There is one thing you can do." The general placed the popcorn bag between them and pulled an envelope from his inside jacket pocket. "Open it."

Stiletto slit the envelope and drew the paper out halfway. It was the address of a woman named Susan LaRochelle.

"Who is she?"

"My niece," the general said. "She's an FBI agent in New York who was covering the US end of the Zubarev shooting. State Department got involved and pulled the plug, but not before she got some information you might like."

"You want me to fly to New York?"

"Yes."

"Is that an order, sir?"

"Consider it the last one I'll ever give you."

CHAPTER 13

THE FLIGHT to New York seemed long. Stiletto stared blankly out the window, unaware of much that was going on around him. Even a screaming baby didn't disturb him.

He might have sounded confident about striking off on his own to take on the battles nobody else would, but he also wondered who he was kidding. That was no way to live, but he had to at least try. Maybe a few months, or a year. If it didn't work, he'd call Ali in San Francisco.

And he'd miss the CIA. With all of its faults, the Agency had been home for a long time, and he had friends there who, presumably, were wondering about him after seeing a stranger clean out his desk. The gossip would be huge, but his phone hadn't rung with anybody asking how he was doing.

The only thing to do right now was stay the course.

He landed at JFK and used his cell to call Susan LaRochelle, who agreed to meet him at her apartment that night. Stiletto checked into a hotel and took a long walk to try to clear his head. When that didn't work, he found a bar and nursed a beer.

Susan met him on time and had Chinese food waiting. Over dinner, they talked about General Ike, her work on the Zubarev case, and the file she'd been presented with before the State Department had pulled the plug on her investigation. He listened with rapt attention to her story about the woman, Siyana Antonova, whom she believed had pulled the trigger on the Zubarevs.

The information in the file confirmed a lot of the information Ravkin's file had contained, except for the names of the local Mob players. Stiletto wanted to know where they were. Susan said the top dog was Shishkin Pavlovitch, and she knew where they hung out.

Scott spent two days tracking the local bosses and finally settled on a plan. Pavlovitch and his buddies liked to play poker in the basement of one of their bars. Finding a back way in was easy. Stiletto contacted Number One and asked for some equipment.

It was time to get even, if only a little.

He heard them laughing as he moved down the hall.

Stiletto gripped the submachine gun a little too tightly. He'd probably over-oiled it, given the residue dripping onto his gloves, but the weapon would not fail. He'd trained and planned too hard for anything to fail now, but deep down he knew he might not survive the night even if he did succeed. If he saw the sunrise, he might live to be an old man.

The dark hallway seemed to close in, the only illumination coming from the crack underneath the door ahead of him. He pushed the jitters away. The walls were not going to crush him. He had to stay focused.

The laughter from behind the door continued. Stiletto adjusted his grip and stepped closer. Sweat coated his skin, his clothes clinging to his body. A trickle down the back of his neck irritated him, and he almost wanted to stop and swipe it away, but he kept his eyes focused on the door.

The laughter stopped, and four voices reached his ears.

"I'll take three."

"One for me."

"I'm good."

"How about we start over?"

More laughing.

Stiletto counted down. Three. Two...

He lifted his booted right foot and slammed it into the wood. The loud thud shook the walls, but the door did not open. He kicked again. Another loud thud and the doorframe started to splinter. Stiletto put everything he had behind the third kick, and the door swung open with enough force to slam into the wall, the collision sounding more like a gunshot than those that followed from the mouth of the submachine gun.

Stiletto stepped into the room, swinging left. The lone guard was reaching for the light switch when Scott blasted him in the chest and belly, cutting him almost in half. The guard left a smear of red on the wall as he fell. His hand still hit the light switch and plunged the room into darkness, but it was too late. Stiletto's combat senses had already pinpointed the remaining targets.

The SMG spat flame in measured bursts, Stiletto shifting his aim as he took out his targets. The flashes from the muzzle created a mild strobe effect that highlighted the twitching bodies of the four men around the poker table. The chips and cards, splashed with blood and bits of flesh, were no longer the center of attention, and the four men saw their lives flashing before them in the strobe. They screamed and cursed, arms flailing, their overweight bodies falling to the floor with squishy finality. When the SMG clicked empty, Stiletto reached for the light switch. One man still lived, his cries of pain filling the room as the echo of the shots faded from Scott's ears.

Stiletto pulled the magazine from the submachine gun and inserted a spare, then stepped into the carnage, doing his best to avoid the puddles of blood although some of it still stuck to the heels of his shoes. He walked around the table to the far side, where the survivor lay on his back, legs and belly torn open by the 9mm flesh-shredders, his bloody fingers clawing for the holstered revolver under his left arm. The tips of those fingers, wet with what was leaking from the man's body, could not wrap around the butt.

Scott aimed the SMG at Pavlovitch's face, which was round and jowly and had a scarred chin. The eyes, still defiant, were confused.

"Would you like to know why?" Stiletto asked.

Pavlovitch gave up reaching for his gun, and his right arm fell limp across his chest. His gasps were getting shorter.

"The Zubarevs, and two others named Ravkin and Anastasia."

Now those defiant eyes widened and he sucked air sharply.

Flame flashed from the SMG once more, and that jowly face splattered into fragments of flesh and bone that peppered the floor.

THE PETROVA BETRAYAL (SCOTT STILETTO 4)

The Petrova Betrayal is book four in the hard-edged, action thriller series – Scott Stiletto.

When valuable high-tech radar plans are stolen from a U.S. defense contractor, chaos breaks loose as friends and enemies snipe at each other to acquire the data.

Scott Stiletto's mission is to retrieve the plans before they fall into the wrong hands, and potentially render the U.S. stealth fleet useless.

The enemy wants to spill blood. Stiletto will make certain it's their own.

A must read for fans of spy-thrillers in the James Bond and Ethan Hunt style.

AVAILABLE JULY 2019 FROM Brian Drake AND WOLFPACK PUBLISHING

A twenty-five year veteran of radio and television broadcasting, Brian Drake has spent his career in San Francisco where he's filled writing, producing, and reporting duties with stations such as KPIX-TV, KCBS, KQED, among many others. Currently carrying out sports and traffic reporting duties for Bloomberg 960, Brian Drake spends time between reports and carefully guarded morning and evening hours cranking out action/adventure tales. A love of reading when he was younger inspired him to create his own stories, and he sold his first short story, "The Desperate Minutes," to an obscure webzine when he was 25 (more years ago than he cares to remember, so don't ask). Many more short story sales followed before he expanded to novels, entering the self-publishing field in 2010, and quickly building enough of a following to attract the attention of several publishers and other writing professionals. Brian Drake lives in California with his wife and two cats, and when he's not writing he is usually blasting along the back roads in his Corvette with his wife telling him not to drive so fast, but the engine is so loud he usually can't hear her.

You will find him regularly blogging at
www.briandrake88.blogspot.com

Find more great titles by Brian Drake and Wolfpack Publishing, here:
https://wolfpackpublishing.com/brian-drake/

Made in the USA
Las Vegas, NV
15 November 2020